A YEARLING BOOK

The man with the white teeth glanced in the direction I was pointing. But from the corner of my eye I saw the other Spaniard come toward me. Running Bird screamed and fled across the meadow and screamed a second time. The Spaniard who had asked me the question caught her long before she reached the trail. Suddenly there was a cloth in my mouth and my hands were behind me and tied hard with a thong.

SCOTT O'DELL was one of the most popular, well-loved authors for young people ever. He was a Newbery Award Medal winner, a three-time Newbery Honor Book winner, a two-time winner of the German Jugendbuchpreis, winner of the deGrummond and Regina medals, and a recipient of the Hans Christian Andersen Author Medal, the highest international recognition for a body of work by an author of children's books.

ALSO AVAILABLE IN LAUREL-LEAF BOOKS:

ISLAND OF THE BLUE DOLPHINS, *Scott O'Dell*

ZIA, *Scott O'Dell*

THE BLACK PEARL, *Scott O'Dell*

THE CHOCOLATE WAR, *Robert Cormier*

I AM THE CHEESE, *Robert Cormier*

DRAGONS IN THE WATERS, *Madeleine L'Engle*

MEET THE AUSTINS, *Madeleine L'Engle*

TROUBLING A STAR, *Madeleine L'Engle*

NIGHTJOHN, *Gary Paulsen*

BLUE SKIN OF THE SEA, *Graham Salisbury*

SING DOWN THE MOON

Scott O'Dell

A YEARLING BOOK

For Shauneille and Don Ryder
and their daughters, Lorraine and Natalie

With thanks to Willard Wallace, Professor of History,
Wesleyan University, for reading my manuscript.—P.F.

Published by
Bantam Doubleday Dell Books for Young Readers
a division of
Bantam Doubleday Dell Publishing Group, Inc.
1540 Broadway
New York, New York 10036

ISBN: 0-440-22739-9

Previous Yearling and Laurel-Leaf editions

Reprinted by arrangement with Macmillan, Inc., on behalf of Bradbury Press

Printed in the United States of America

June 1997

10 9 8 7 6 5 4 3 2 1

RAD

Sing Down the Moon

1

On the high Mesas above our canyon spring came early that year. The piñon trees shook off their coverings of snow in the month of the deer. Warm winds melted the snow and blue water gathered under the trees and ran through the meadows and down the steep barrancas. Far to the north, where the stone walls of the canyon stand so close together that you can touch them with your outstretched hands, the waters met and flowed toward the south, past Spider Rock and Lost Sheep Mountain, at last in a big loop past our village.

The day the waters came was a wonderful day.

I heard the first sounds of their coming while I lay awake in the night. At first it was a whisper, like a wind among the dry stalks of our cornfield. After a while it was a sound like the feet of warriors dancing. Then it was a roar that shook the earth. I could hardly wait until the sun rose.

When the first light showed in the east, I hurried out to see the river running. My father and mother and my sister, Lapana, had seen early springs many times before, so they were sleeping.

I stood alone in the orchard, where the peaches grow. It was a miracle. Yesterday there was nothing to see save bare trees and wide stretches of yellow sand. In one night everything had changed. The trees had begun to bud and the sand lay deep under blue, rushing water.

I felt like singing. I wanted to leap and dance with joy, yet I stood quietly and watched the river running between the greening cottonwood trees, for I knew that it is bad luck to be so happy. The gods do not like anyone to show happiness in this way and they punish those who do not obey them. They punished my brother. They let the lightning strike him when he was coming home from a hunt. My brother had shot a six-pronged deer and was singing because it was the first deer with six prongs that anyone had shot that summer. The lightning struck him and he died.

Thinking of my brother, I stood quiet. No one could tell how I felt. Yet it was hard for me to do. It was very hard because now that spring had come I would have another chance to take our sheep up the long trail to the mesa.

I had driven them there once before, last year on the day the waters began to run. But it was a bad time for me. I thought of that spring now. It was not so hard any longer to stand quiet and think about it.

I was happy going up the trail that day last spring, with sheep bells ringing and the sheep white in their winter coats, hungry to reach spring pasture. When we left the trail it was fun to see them scatter out over the meadow to crop the first young grass, as though they had never eaten in their lives.

It was fun all morning and some of the afternoon. Then white clouds came up, but after a while they turned black. It was then that I should have left the meadow and driven the flock down the trail to home. This I should have done, as any good shepherd knows. What I did was wrong. I waited, thinking that the black clouds would go away or that if a storm came it would be a small one.

The storm was not small. At first it only rained and I herded the flock into an aspen grove for shelter against the wind that had grown cold. Then it began to snow.

I had never been afraid before, or only once. That was when I saw my grandfather, who had been dead for a long time, walking around. It was night just like the one last spring, with snow and a cold wind blowing. He came right out of the trees and the falling snow and walked toward me and called my name.

That happened when I was ten years old. Now that I was fourteen, I should not have been afraid, but I was. I thought about how warm it would be in our house that has thick mud walls and a door so small you have to crawl on your hands and knees to go through it. The sheep were safe under the shelter of the aspen trees. They would not freeze in their thick wool coats and in the morning I would come back.

I left them and went down the trail. At the bottom of the canyon the snow was not falling. I crawled through the door. My father and mother and my sister, who were sitting around the fire, looked at me—at my muddy feet and wet clothes and my long hair that was covered with snow. They knew something was wrong.

Lapana, my sister, said, "We could see the storm gathering on the mesa."

Lapana was only two years older than I, but she talked as though she were ten years older.

"We thought you would come home before the storm," my father said.

"Where are the sheep?" my mother said.

She thought of the sheep because they were hers. In the tribe I belong to, the Navahos, sheep are mostly owned by the women. It was right, therefore, that she should think of the sheep first.

"They are safe," I said.

"Where?" Lapana said.

"I am listening," my mother said, "but I hear no sheep bells."

All of them knew that I had left the sheep on the mesa, though they did not know why.

"The sheep are in the aspen grove," I said.

"You left them because you got scared," Lapana said. "The storm scared you."

My mother said nothing. She rose from the fire and found two blankets and put one around her shoulders and gave the other to me. She went outside and I followed her. We crossed the stream and climbed the trail. Snow was still falling on the mesa, but the sheep were safe, deep in the aspen grove. We cleared a place and sat down near them and wrapped ourselves in the blankets. It was a long night because my mother did not speak to me.

Nor did she speak when morning came and we drove the flock down the trail and across the river, into the brush corral. Nor did she ever speak of that night, but all the rest of the spring and during the summer and fall she would not let me take the flock to the mesa.

Now a new spring had come. I could not wait until my mother was awake and I could ask her about the sheep.

2

I did not have to wait long and I had no need to tell my mother that another spring had come and I wanted to take the sheep to the mesa. Nor say that I had learned in the days between the two springs that a herder of sheep does not leave the flock to fend for itself, whether from fear of storms or wild animals or for any reason. She was waiting at the gate of the corral when I came back from the river.

"The grass is better to the south, beyond the aspen grove," she said. "It is still watery and thin, but the sheep will find it good after a winter of mesquite."

She gave me a strip of dried deer to eat at noon and waited while I drove the sheep out of the corral and across the river. As I reached the trail, she waved to me.

The trail to the mesa is steep and follows a wooded draw and then cuts back and forth for a long time. It is the only trail out of the canyon for a distance of two leagues. Our men use it when they go scouting or go to hunt. Because the trail is steep, it is easy to defend if warriors from the west come to raid our canyon.

We reached the mesa when the sun was lance high in the east, long before the other girls from our village came, which pleased me. The sheep were cropping the short grass and my dog sat watching when White Deer came up the trail with her flock. I smiled and welcomed her, which was my right because I had been the first to reach the mesa. We both smiled and greeted Running Bird, who did not come until most of the grass had been cropped from the south meadow.

But at noon the three of us ate together, while our flocks grazed.

"Have you heard," said Running Bird, "that the twins are ill?"

"They are always ill," White Deer said.

"Neither of them has any strength," Running Bird said. "It would be wiser if there was only one of the twins instead of two. There is not enough strength to divide between them."

"Would you like to have twin babies when you are married?" White Deer said to me.

"I have never thought of this," I said, not telling the truth.

"She thinks of it all the time," Running Bird said.

"She is too thin to have twins," White Deer said.

"She is thin because she eats nothing," said Running Bird.

They were joking with me. I am not thin and I eat a lot. My sister says that I eat like a man. But this joking is our custom. Only yesterday my father got a new horse. When he jumped on its back and rode proudly back and forth to show off, my uncle laughed.

"Your feet touch the ground," he said. "Either the legs of your new horse are too short or your legs, dear brother, are too long."

We like to joke with each other in this way, so I was not displeased at what my two friends said about me. I thought of something to pay them back, but before I could say it Running Bird spoke.

"It is possible that our friend will never be married," she said. "Who wants a girl who has arms that look like sticks?"

"Oh," White Deer said, "some poor man may marry her. He will see that she eats little and think it will not matter whether he is poor or not."

"More likely he will see that her mother owns many sheep," Running Bird said.

"Yes, most young men dream of mothers-in-law with many sheep," White Deer said.

"But I do not think that Tall Boy is one of these dreamers," Running Bird said. "Do you?"

I was a healthy girl and good at weaving, but I was not pretty like my two friends. Many people thought that the only reason Tall Boy's parents wanted him to marry me was because my mother owned many sheep.

"It does not matter what others think," White Deer said. "Tall Boy will marry her only because she is pretty and obedient."

"And eats so little," Running Bird said.

My sheep were grazing nearby. I listened to the sound of their teeth as they sheared the long grass. I looked up at the sky which was blue and listened to the far-off sound of moving water. My friends waited for me to answer them. They wanted me to talk about Tall Boy, who in the morning would be riding west with our warriors.

White Deer grew impatient at my silence. "Tall Boy is very brave," she said.

"Sometimes he is too brave," Running Bird said.

They were goading me to speak, but still I kept silent. I got up and caught one of my sheep that was straying and chased it back into the flock. When I sat down again my friends were whispering to each other. They acted as though I was not there.

"In the land of the Utes, the girls are beautiful," White Deer said. "I have heard this from my father and brothers who have traveled there."

"It is true," said Running Bird. "Once I saw a girl from that land. I was a child then, yet I have never forgotten."

"Perhaps Tall Boy will bring one home," White Deer said.

"It is possible," said Running Bird.

I raised my knees under my chin and rested my chin on them and watched the flocks grazing. After a while I said to White Deer, "Three of your sheep have strayed." To Running Bird I said, "One of yours is eating poison weed." Then I felt better.

3

Early the next morning our young warriors left for the west country. They gathered in the night, riding from their homes nearby. All night they danced and sang and beat on drums. It was a big wonder that they had enough strength left to climb into their saddles when daylight came. But as I went out to build the breakfast fire, they sat astride their horses, ready to leave.

There were twelve warriors. They wore red paint and in their hair gray eagle feathers. Tall Boy, the leader, rode among them, making certain that everything was in order. I glanced up at him as I stirred the supper ashes alive and set fresh wood. Cedar smoke rose and drifted across the meadow. He must have smelled it, but he did not glance in my direction. He looked very tall in the dim light.

I thought what a good name he had taken for himself. It was better than his first name, River Boy, which his father had given him. He had carried it now for two springs and a summer, since the day he killed the brown bear beyond Rainbow Mountain. He had brought the skin home and said

Tall Boy had taken it, pointing to himself. After that, everybody called him by this name.

With the first flash of sun on the canyon wall, the men rode out of the meadow. Tall Boy led the way, moving briskly on his white pony. He did not look to either side, nor at those who had come to wish the warriors farewell, nor at me. He looked straight in front of him, his bold chin thrust out and his mouth drawn tight.

My mother watched him go by, then she said, "I hope that he does not kill another bear. If he does he will call himself Very Tall Boy and we will have much trouble with him."

My mother did not like him, but I did not mind his haughty ways. For his sake I wished he would kill another bear.

The warriors reached the end of the meadow and Tall Boy led them across the stream. On the far bank he turned for a moment and glanced over his shoulder, then raised his hand. I thought he might be waving at me, so I waved back. I watched until he disappeared and the sound of hoofs died away.

After breakfast I drove my sheep to the mesa. White Deer and Running Bird were already there with their flocks. When the sheep had settled down we sat under a tree and talked about the warriors. We talked and laughed together all the morning. At noon the two girls left to move their flocks.

An eagle was soaring overhead on a wind that did not blow here on the mesa and I watched until it drifted out of sight. A herd of white-tailed antelope came to graze among my sheep. I was driving them away when I heard Running Bird call. She was standing on a ledge that jutted out over the canyon. She pointed down, down with two quick thrusts of her hand. As I ran toward her I heard the sound of a gun.

I went to the ledge where she stood and gazed down into the canyon.

Far below, moving along the river, was a line of horsemen. There were ten of them. They were not Indians. They carried long rifles slung to their saddles and their hats were broad brimmed and turned up at one side. They were white soldiers who lived to the south of our canyon, at Fort Defiance. I knew them because they had ridden through our canyon on a day last summer.

"What shall we do?" Running Bird said. She was frightened. "Shall we hide?"

I was frightened, too, but I said calmly, "No, let us stay here and watch."

"Last summer they threatened to come back and burn our village," Running Bird said. "They are back."

"They would burn our village if we did not keep the peace is what they told us. We have kept the peace."

"But our warriors are away now on a raid," said Running Bird.

"They have gone to raid our enemies, the Utes," I said. "That is different from raiding the white men."

As we watched, the first of the soldiers came to the village. He got off his horse and went to the hogan where Old Bear lived. Dogs were barking but there was no other sound in the village. Then Old Bear came out of the hogan and greeted the soldier and they went inside. The other soldiers sat on their horses and waited, with their rifles held across their laps. On the barrels of their rifles were fastened long, sharp-looking knives. That is why we always called them the Long Knives.

The sun crawled up the sky. It was a long time before the Long Knife came out of the hogan. We watched while he mounted his horse and the ten rode away, one by one out of the canyon. Not until they were far out on the plain, until they were a small cloud of dust, did my people come out of their houses.

Running Bird said, "I want to go down and learn what the Long Knife told Old Bear."

She grasped my arm. I held back, remembering the time I had left the sheep when the storm came.

"You go," I said. "I will watch your sheep until you return."

She ran across the meadow and disappeared. I heard the clatter of stones as she went down the trail. Her sheep were wandering and with the help of my black dog I gathered them in. Running Bird did not return until it was time to drive the sheep home. She was out of breath from the long climb and did not speak until we were halfway down the trail. I had to ask her twice what the Long Knife had said to Old Bear before she answered me.

"He asked Old Bear," she said, " 'where are your warriors?' Old Bear told him that they were in the north, hunting in the North Country. And the Long Knife said that was good, but if they were not hunting, if he learned that they were on a raid somewhere, he would come back and burn the houses and kill everyone in the village. Even the women and children he would kill, even the sheep and the dogs. That was the last thing he said to Old Bear."

"What did Old Bear say?" I asked her.

"He said that he would keep the peace. He would keep it unless our village was attacked by the Utes or the Spaniards or our other enemies. Then he would fight as he had fought before when they had come to plunder us."

"I hope Tall Boy does not raid among the Utes," I said.

"Or if he does," White Deer said, "the soldiers will never hear of it."

We had reached the stream and the sheep were wading toward the far shore. Suddenly Running Bird put her arm around my waist.

"Tall Boy is very brave but not foolhardy," Running Bird said. "He will come back safely and he will not bring back a Ute girl. You will see that I am right."

She gave me a squeeze and we walked on through the river in silence. Dusk was falling and blue smoke rose from all the hogans. I drove my sheep into the corral and closed the gate and sang to myself as I walked homeward.

4

Our hogan was quiet that night. All the hogans in our village were quiet. The Long Knives' threat hung over us. Had our young warriors been home there would have been much talk and chanting and threats against the Long Knives. But there were only women and children who had nothing to say and old men who had seen the power of the white man and feared it.

The evening fires went out early. The night was long and I was glad when dawn came. At the first gray light I opened the gate and drove the sheep across the river and up the trail. As the sheep bells tinkled in the silent canyon, I sang little songs to myself. Some were happy and some were not, but all of them were meant for the ears of the gods who listen.

When I reached the mesa the sky was gold along the edges and pink overhead. With my black dog I drove the flock beyond the aspen grove to a place where the grass was uncropped.

Running Bird came soon and the two flocks grazed together. My sheep were easy to find because they were marked with red dye, a red circle on each ear. That afternoon when the sun was hot I would make the ten sheep my mother had given me, using two red circles to show that they were mine.

Running Bird began to talk about the soldiers. I listened to her, nodding and making polite sounds, but I was thinking about my sheep all the time. The ewes my mother had given me would lamb in the summer. When spring came again I might have twenty or thirty sheep of my own to drive to the mesa. Thirty sheep! The thought made me dizzy with happiness. Right at the moment Running Bird asked me what my father had said about the soldiers I jumped up and began to dance. I could not help it, thinking of thirty sheep grazing in the meadow, each one with two red circles on its ears.

Clouds drifted in from the north, but they were spring clouds, white as lamb's wool. In the stream that wandered across the mesa speckled trout were leaping. Jays were chattering in the aspen trees and two little red-tailed hawks came and hovered over the meadow.

It was the barking of my black dog that first alarmed me. None of the sheep had strayed. Everything was peaceful in the meadow. There was no reason for him to bark. Then, close to the aspen grove, I saw two long shadows.

I saw their shadows before I saw the men. They were not soldiers because they did not wear bright buttons on their coats and bright cloths around their necks. They were dressed in deerskin, with tall hats and silver spurs, riding horses that had heavy silver bits. They were Spaniards.

I jumped to my feet. They rode up at a trot and reined in a few paces away. The one who spoke had a soft voice and many white teeth and long black hair.

"A fine day," he said, "but we are lost. Which is the quick way to Corn Mountain?"

I knew little Spanish then, not so much as I do now, yet I understood him. I pointed to the northwest and said that there was a trail near the rim of the canyon and that Corn Mountain was two leagues beyond as the eagle flies.

While I was saying this, I saw something that I should have seen before. The other Spaniard held the reins of two horses, which he had been leading. Their saddles were empty and I knew in the time a breath takes that these men were slavers. For many years now they had come to the Navaho country and stolen girls to sell to families in the town who needed girls to cook for them and to wash their floors. One of the Navaho girls had escaped and come back to Canyon de Chelly and told us what had happened to her.

The man with the white teeth glanced in the direction I was pointing. But from the corner of my eye I saw the other Spaniard come toward me. Running Bird screamed and fled across the meadow and screamed a second time. The Spaniard who had asked me the question caught her long before she reached the trail. Suddenly there was a cloth in my mouth and my hands were behind me and tied hard with a thong.

My black dog was rushing around, barking and nipping at their heels. The Spaniard who had a flatshaped head and a yellow scar on his chin struck him with a rifle and he lay still. Then they put us on the two horses they had bought and tied our hands to the saddle horns.

"We will not harm you," the Spaniard with the white teeth said. "You will like the place you are going. Do not try to flee."

We went south along the mesa. As we passed the head of the trail, I looked for White Deer, hoping that she would be coming up with her flock and would see us. I saw no one. We took the Dawn Trail to the lowlands and at dusk reached the river, far below our village.

5

We left the canyon at a fast trot and did not halt until shadows began to lengthen. We rested beside a stream while the night gathered. The Spaniards made a small fire and warmed corncakes. They offered Running Bird and me some of the food, but we said that we were not hungry.

All of the time we were there by the stream they kept their eyes on us. Often they would stop whatever they were doing to listen for the sound of hoofs. They did not know that all of our young warriors were away in the west and only the old men were left in the village.

A thin moon came up. We started off again, going southward into the country I did not know, through scattered groves of piñon pine and low hills deep in grass. Running Bird and I rode close together, sometimes holding hands for comfort. At first we were too frightened to speak, but as the night wore on we began to plan how we would escape from the Spaniards. They were riding in front of us and whenever they talked we had a chance to whisper to each other.

"They will have to sleep sometime," Running Bird said, "and then we can flee."

"If they hobble the horses," I said, "we can go on foot."

"It is better on foot," Running Bird whispered. "We can hide easier without the horses."

"We must go the first chance we have," I said.

"Soon," Running Bird whispered. "At dawn if we can."

When the moon set and it was too dark to travel, the Spaniards halted again. We thought that our chance to flee had come, but the men before they laid down to sleep bound Running Bird and me with leather thongs, tying our hands and feet so that we could not stand or crawl, or scarcely move.

The Spaniards slept until the sun was high. They offered us water, which we drank, and cold corncakes. The man with the flat head did not like it that we would not eat the cakes and threatened us with a stick. Still we did not eat.

We traveled until dark and waited for the moon to rise and started off once more into the south, riding along a dim trail through open country. Just as the moon went down, I heard a sound behind us. I looked quickly over my shoulder. There on the low rise we had climbed a moment before I saw what I was sure was a Wolf, a Navaho Wolf.

Running Bird saw it too, but she said nothing.

We were too fearful to speak, for these Wolves are sometimes witches. They are humans who dress up as wolves and try to do you harm. I was too far away to see its long claws and sharp fangs.

Soon after the moon set we halted and made camp. Neither Running Bird nor I saw the Wolf again, though we stayed awake and looked for him and listened.

6

We went south for three suns. I knew it was south because the North Star was behind us. We traveled at night and slept in the daytime, always away from the trail. During the day while they slept, the Spaniards tied Running Bird and me together. At night they let us ride free, but there was no chance to escape and we did not try.

At dawn when the fourth sun rose my black dog was sitting under a tree close to where Running Bird and I lay. I was overjoyed to see him, having thought he was dead. He would not have left the sheep alone, so I knew that my mother had come to the mesa and driven the flock home.

When the Spaniard with the flat head awoke and saw the black dog there under the tree he wanted to shoot him. But the other Spaniard made the man put his gun away.

"These Navahos are happy with their dogs," he said. "Happy girls bring better prices than unhappy girls. That I have learned and do not need to learn again."

The fourth night when the moon was overhead,

I saw dim lights in the distance and soon we came to a place where white people lived. There was a wide street with many houses along it and many trees in a row.

"My grandfather came to this place once," Running Bird whispered to me. "I think it was this place. He said that he saw more houses than a dog has fleas. They were close together and painted different colors and there were trees in front of the houses. He gave it a name but I have forgotten."

The two Spaniards stopped at the edge of the town and untied us and told us to get down from the horses. They led us to a hut among the trees and knocked on the door. An old woman came, clutching a candle in a bony hand. With her other hand she snatched me inside. Then she snatched Running Bird. Then the two Spaniards rode away.

The old woman was a Jicarilla Apache and did not understand us when we spoke. The Apaches and Navahos were blood brothers once, but she shook her head and did not answer. In the middle of the hut a fire was burning under a pot of thick stew. Steam came up from the pot and a strong odor stung my nose.

"It is dog meat," I said to Running Bird.

"Yes, it is dog and an old one," she said.

The woman started to fill two bowls with the stew. By signs I told her that we had eaten and were not hungry. I did not try to tell her that my people, the Navahos, never ate stew made of dog meat.

The old woman spread a blanket on the floor for Running Bird and me to sleep on. Then she spread a blanket for herself and lay down in front of the door, so that we could not open it. I was tired, but I did not sleep. I made my black dog lie down beside me. I had seen the old woman eyeing him and I was afraid that if I went to sleep she would kill him to make a stew.

Early the next morning the Spaniard with the white teeth came back. He gave the old woman a silver coin, which she hid in her mouth. Then he motioned me to follow him. Running Bird held on to me until the Spaniard pulled us apart. I did not know what to say to her. I went out of the hut and the Spaniard got on his horse and I followed him, the black dog walking beside me.

As we left the hut, the old woman hobbled after us and threw a leather rope around the dog's neck and tried to drag him back.

The Spaniard wheeled his horse around. "Let the dog loose," he said, "I will bring you another, a fatter one."

The old woman did as she was told and the three of us left her and went down the street.

There was no one around. When we were almost at the end of the street I saw a girl sweeping the earth in front of a gate. She was an Indian and had the marks of the Nez Percé on her cheeks. She glanced up at me, though she did not stop her sweeping. It was a quick glance, yet in it was something that chilled me. As if she were saying, "Run, run, even though they kill you. It is better to die here on the street."

7

At the last house on the street, the Spaniard tied his horse to a tree and pulled on a rope that hung above an iron gate. Bells sounded far off and an Indian girl came running to let us in. What tribe she belonged to I could not tell, but she was smiling and looked happier than the Nez Percé girl.

There was a large place inside the wall where bright flowers were growing. A path led through them and we followed it and went into a big kitchen at the back of the house. Strings of peppers hung from the rafters, some red, some green, and loops of white onions. Two big pots of beans were bubbling on a stove.

"Are you hungry?" the girl asked me in Navaho.

"No," I said, though I had eaten little for five days. I was rude and did not thank her.

After a moment a young woman came into the kitchen. She wore black shoes and a red velvet skirt and a white camisa. She had blue eyes and her hair was the color of corn silk when it begins to ripen in the summer. To my surprise she spoke to me in Navaho, asking me to walk around the kitchen.

My boots were covered with mud and my leggings stained from the long ride. I did not want to walk around the kitchen. Nor did I know why I should, so I stood in the middle of the room and did not move. I thought, if I stand here long enough they will let me go.

"A surly miss," the woman said in Spanish. "Can't you bring me one with a better disposition?"

"She is frightened," the Spaniard said. "In a few days she will act better. Remember that Rosita was this way when I brought her here two years ago. Now look at her."

He glanced at the girl who was stirring the beans with a big spoon. She turned and smiled at him.

I will never stir the beans nor will I ever smile while I am in this house, I said to myself. Then the Spaniard took my arm in a hard grip and led me back and forth from one side of the kitchen to the other. I pulled away from him.

"She walks pigeon-toed," the young woman said.

"They all do," the Spaniard said, "the Kiowas, the Comanches, the Nez Percés, the Zuñis, and the Apaches. All of them."

The woman said, "The Hopis don't walk like a pigeon."

"I will find you a Hopi, maybe in the fall," the Spaniard said, "but now I have a strong girl who is used to hard work."

"I have two strong girls already," the woman answered. "I need one who can meet guests at the door and wait on table."

She walked around me, gently running her hand across my back. Then she asked me to smile and when I refused she reached out and pushed my lips back with her fingers. On one side I have a broken tooth, which happened when I was very young and fell against a stone.

The woman made a sound with her tongue, but said nothing. Then she walked around me once more and left the room with the Spaniard.

The girl, who had opened the gate for us and who was stirring the beans, said, "My name is Rosita. I am twelve years old and I come from the White Mesa, in the Navaho country. What is your name? Where do you come from? How old are you?"

I told her one of my names, but not my real one. "I am fifteen and I come from the Canyon de Chelly."

"I have never heard of that place," Rosita said.

This surprised me, for I thought everyone had heard of the Canyon de Chelly. "It is the most beautiful place in the world," I said. "It has the most sheep and the finest wool. It has a river and tall cliffs that catch the sun and make the melons grow bigger than pumpkins. There the cornstalks grow taller than you are."

I wanted to tell her more about the Canyon de Chelly, but my throat filled up with sadness.

Rosita put a bowl of beans and chili on the table beside me, where I could reach it.

"You will be happy here," she said. "The lady is kind and her husband also. He is a soldier and does not come here often, mostly on feast days. There is good food to eat and the work is not hard. It will be nicer when you are in the house. The other girl I do not like. She is a Zuñi."

From the next room I heard the sound of the woman and the Spaniard talking. They talked like the Anglos who come to our canyon and haggle over the price of wool.

Rosita listened to them for a moment. "The Señora paid little for me," she said. "But for you she will pay more. You are pretty and tall. I wish you were my sister."

After a long time the Spaniard left. He was carrying a leather pouch. It was filled with coins that jingled.

"I told you," Rosita said. "The pouch is twice as full as it was for me."

The woman came and led me out of the kitchen. My black dog was waiting for me. We went along a path to a smaller house far in the back. It had a wide, blue door and inside was a room bigger than our hogan and home, where all my family lived, cooking and weaving rugs and sleeping. The floor was not made of common earth like ours, but of adobe mixed with blood. It was smooth and dark and on it were two Navaho blankets.

"You sleep there," the woman told me, pointing

to a big bed. She spoke to me in Navaho. Her words had a strange sound but I understood them. She opened the doors of an empty cupboard. "For clothes," she said. "Tomorrow I buy you shoes, dresses, and some ribbons for your hair."

She looked down at my black dog, who stood close to me, as close as he could get. "You keep him here," she said. "Not in house. Never in house. Understand?"

I understood. I think the black dog understood, too.

The woman smiled and patted me on the shoulder. Then she closed the door and we left the black dog in the room and went back to the kitchen. She told Rosita to show me what to do. She left the house and I did not see her until suppertime.

Rosita showed me how to set the table, where everything went, and how to light the three candles.

"When the Señora buys you a new dress," Rosita said, "I will show you how to carry the food in and put it on the table."

I waited in the kitchen until the woman finished her supper. Then I took the food she had left back to the kitchen. There was much of it, enough to feed many people, and Rosita said that we could eat all of it we wanted. I ate little because it did not taste good. In the Canyon de Chelly everyone eats at the same time. We eat out of one big pot and we do not use knives or forks, but the food tastes better.

I helped Rosita wash the dishes and she showed me how to put them away in the cupboard, everything in neat rows. When we were ready to sleep she showed me how to get into my bed. I did all the things she told me to, but after she fell asleep I got out of the bed and lay down on the floor. My black dog curled up beside me.

For a long time I lay awake, thinking of the canyon and the mesa and the sheep and my family. I thought about Tall Boy, too. He would come home before spring was ended. He would learn what had befallen me. Surely, he would ride out with his warriors and find me and take me home.

The night was very quiet. I began to wonder what I would do if he did not come home, if he did not come for me. I would steal away. Some night Running Bird and I would go together. We would travel at night and hide in the daytime, like the Spaniards had done.

An owl flew into a tree outside the window. He was silent for a long time and then he began to make churring sounds, the same sounds that the owls made at home. It was a good omen.

8

Three mornings later the woman took me to the store and bought me two dresses, one of wool and one of velveteen, and a pair of red shoes with buttons on them. She forgot to buy me a ribbon for my hair. I said nothing because I would not need a ribbon for very long. When the next full moon came I would not be there to use it. When the moon was light enough to see by, Running Bird and I would steal away and take the road to home.

Where Running Bird was, I did not know. I asked Rosita if she had heard about her. I looked for her as the woman and I walked up the street and in the store I kept watching, and on the way back. I did not find out where she was until the day after the first new moon.

Rosita and I went to the market on that morning to buy vegetables. While she was picking out a basket of chilies, going over each one carefully because the Señora would punish her if she brought any back that were scarred, I left her and walked around through the market in the hope that I might see Running Bird.

There were many Indian girls there, a dozen maybe, but I did not see Running Bird. I had given up and was on my way back to where Rosita stood when I heard a sound behind me. It was the Nez Percé, the one who was sweeping under the trees the morning the Spaniard brought me into the town.

She held up a basket of things she had and I thought that she wanted to show them to me. But as I looked at them, she said quickly in a low voice, "Do not trust Rosita. Everything you tell her she will tell the Señora. There is a baile at your house to night. My Señora is sending me to help you get the house ready, me and another girl. Your friend lives in the second house near the market. It has an iron gate and a pole with a flag on it. My name is Nehana."

The girl said this in one breath and was gone before I could answer.

Rosita had three baskets filled with food. We each carried one and shared the other. As we left the market I looked for the house where Running Bird was. I saw the big iron gate and the flag on the pole, but the gate was closed and there was a lock on it. I did not tell Rosita that the Nez Percé girl had spoken to me.

The three baskets of food we carried back to the house were for the party the Señora had that night. The rest of the day I spent peeling chili peppers. I burned the skins over a fire and scraped them off and split each pod. Then I picked out the hundreds of little white seeds and placed the pods on a platter. Now and again the Señora came and watched me, to make me hurry, I guess.

I did not hurry, yet by late afternoon I had done six platters of chili peppers. My fingers were on fire and I could scarcely see from my eyes. Nehana, the Nez Percé girl, was there, as she said she would be, sweeping the house and the walks and cutting flowers to put in bowls. She acted as if she had never seen me and when I spoke to her she did not answer.

After I finished with the chili peppers the Señora sent me off to my room to put on the new button shoes and the velveteen dress.

People came when the sun went down. They filled the house and flowed out into the garden. In my new clothes I walked around among them, as I was told, carrying a big tray of food. When one tray was empty I went back to the kitchen for another.

Most of the men were Long Knives. They were like the men who had come to our canyon and threatened to destroy our crops and burn our hogans. The Señora had told me to smile as I passed the food around, but I hated everyone there, the soldiers and their wives, too, and I did not obey her.

I saw Nehana many times while I was in the kitchen or walking around with trays of food, but she never spoke. Once when Rosita noticed that I was looking at the girl, she cautioned me.

"That one you keep looking at," she said, "is

bad. Once last year she ran away. She was caught and beaten for it, with a long leather whip. If she talks to you, do not listen. If the Señora catches you talking to her, you will be punished."

During the days I had been a slave in the house, I had learned that Rosita liked the life she was living. She came from a poor tribe and a poor family and she liked all the food she got to eat, the clothes the Señora bought for her, the soft bed, and the big room. She liked ordering me around and the penny she always got to keep when she went to the market.

If she talks to me, I wanted to say, I will talk to her, whether I am punished or not.

"You will be happy here someday," Rosita said.

Most of the people were leaving and I was in the kitchen. Nehana was bringing dishes in for me to wash. Rosita and another girl were helping the women put on their cloaks. Nehana put a tray of dishes on the table and started out of the kitchen.

She turned at the door and listened. Men on horses were riding away. Someone was playing a guitar in the garden. Women were laughing in the other part of the house.

"In ten days," Nehana said, holding up ten fingers, "at the church."

The next instant she was gone and I went on washing the dishes. There were many. Rosita and I worked until the first roosters crowed. When we went to our room I lay down on the floor as I had every night since I came. But I did not sleep until gray light showed through the window.

9

On the tenth night after the baile Rosita and I went to the church. I tried to go alone, for this was the night Nehana had told me to come, but the Señora went with us.

While we were walking up the street she asked Rosita to tell me about the fiesta.

"It is called Easter," Rosita said, and told me all she had learned during the time she had been a slave—how Jesús Cristo was placed upon a wooden cross and slain and then how he rose from the dead.

"Jesús Cristo," Rosita said, "is like all our gods if you put them together. He is Falling Water and Spider Woman. But he is not cunning like Falling Water, nor is he vengeful like Spider Woman."

I nodded my head as though I understood everything she said, but I was not listening. I wondered if Nehana would come to the church, if she would see the three of us together and leave without speaking to me. I also wondered where Tall Boy was, if even now he was hidden somewhere near, waiting to take me home. I wondered so hard that I stumbled in a hole and fell down. I got dirt on my new velveteen dress and scuffed my red button shoes, which made the Señora angry.

The door of the church was covered with pine boughs and inside there were flowers everywhere. Smoke rose in the air. It smelled sweet as it swirled about me. The church was crowded with people, and though I kept glancing around while children dressed in white gowns were singing, I did not see Nehana.

When the singing and the talk were over we went out with the others. Nehana stood near the door, all but her eyes covered with a shawl. I was walking behind Rosita and the Señora. Nehana turned her back and waited for them to pass. Then she glanced at me. She was a dozen steps away and many people were around her, but I saw her hold up one finger, as she had held up ten the night of the baile. That is all she did before she disappeared, but I was sure that she meant for me to come there the following night.

On the way back to the house, the Señora asked me if I liked the fiesta. I said, "Yes," which seemed to please her. I began to plan how I would get to the church alone on the following night.

The next morning, when Rosita was not looking, I wrapped twenty tortillas in a cloth, ten for me and ten for the black dog, and hid them in my room. When it was time for me to help with the supper I told Rosita that I had a headache and went to bed.

The Señora came and gave me a spoonful of

something out of a bottle, which choked me but I did not mind. As soon as she left, I jumped up and got my blanket and the bundle of tortillas. I closed the door and walked quietly along the path to the front of the house.

The gate was locked. I had forgotten that the Señora locked it each night. The adobe wall that surrounded the house was higher than my head and the top was covered with pieces of broken glass. I stood there looking at it. I heard the Señora's voice and the closing of a door somewhere.

In a panic I threw the tortillas over the wall, then the blanket. The blanket caught on the pieces of glass and hung there. This was fortunate for me because I was able to put the black dog on top of the wall and climb up after him. I jumped to the ground. The dog followed me and we ran. I took my blanket but I forgot the tortillas.

People were going into the church. Nehana came out of the shadows and with her was Running Bird. Nehana did not go in but went past the door and along the side of the church. We followed her, walking carefully in the dark. We came to a ditch where water was flowing ankle deep and ran along it.

We traveled for a long time in darkness. Then the moon rose and we came to a path, which we followed to the ridge of a low hill. Below us in a small valley, I saw a clump of cottonwood trees, lights winking among them, and nearby the outlines of a building. While we stood there, catching our breath, men and women on horseback passed us and rode down toward the lights.

"That is where the Penitentes meet," Nehana said. "I do not belong to them but they will not harm us. It is far from town so the Penitentes come here on their horses. There will be many horses for us to choose from. Without horses they would catch us before we went far, as they caught me once."

When we reached the cottonwood trees, Nehana told Running Bird and me to put the blankets over our heads so that only our eyes showed.

Many horses were tethered in the cottonwood grove, some hobbled, some tied to the trees. Nehana went slowly, looking at them as we passed. Most of them were fine horses and had bridles made of silver and turquoise. A few men were standing among the trees smoking, and a crowd was gathered in front of the church, which was long and narrow like the white man's coffin.

"I have chosen three good horses," Nehana whispered as we left the grove. "But to take them now is unwise. We must wait for the right time. The three horses are pintos and they are tethered near the far side of the grove."

Running Bird and I followed her into the church and stood in the back, near the door.

"I will tell you when to leave," she whispered. "It will be when they put out the candles and everything is dark. Do not speak and keep your faces hidden. When I go, follow me quickly."

Half the people in the church were women and

they held lighted candles. The men carried leather whips tipped with pieces of iron. Everyone stood quietly, facing the altar. Clouds of sweet-smelling smoke drifted back and forth. It was very hot and hard to breathe, but I kept my head covered.

At the far end of the church a drum began to beat. Someone played on a flute softly and a bent old man spoke a verse and people joined him, repeating what he said.

A tall figure suddenly appeared at the door, a man with a circle of cactus thorns around his head. He was carrying a heavy wooden cross on his back. On his face there were spots of blood.

Nehana grasped my arm. I felt her body grow stiff beside me. As I looked at the man standing in the doorway, his mouth began to move in pain and I saw a flash of white teeth.

"The Spaniard," Nehana whispered. "The slave catcher."

We stood tight against the wall, holding each other by the hand. The Spaniard looked one way and the other, peering through the candle smoke at everyone, at us. I did not breathe. At last he looked away and began to stagger toward the far end of the church, as people made way for him.

"They think he is Jesús Cristo," Nehana whispered.

He reached the far wall and two men took the cross from his back and a man held him so he would not fall. The flute started to play again. Someone gave a loud cry, like the cry of a wounded animal, and all the candles, as if there were only one, went out at the same time.

While the darkness settled down around us, there was a time of awful silence. Then women began to weep and louder than the weeping came the sound of whips whistling through the air, striking again and again.

Nehana pulled at my dress and the three of us squirmed our way through the darkness and found the door. Nehana ran toward the cottonwood trees and we followed her, the black dog at my heels. Nehana did not pause. She ran toward the three pintos tethered at the far edge of the grove.

The moon was high in the east. We got into the saddles and rode toward it, moving slowly through the mesquite until the sound of weeping and the crack of whips died away in the night.

10

Nehana led the way along a trail that wound downward toward a small pine forest. We had not gone far when we saw a fire burning at the edges of the trees. Nehana pulled in her horse and sat watching.

"Woodcutters use this trail," she said. "One of them must be camped there now. It is not good if he sees us. But we cannot go back. Nor can we get through the forest without using the trail."

Slowly she rode on and we followed her. "If he tries to stop us," Nehana said, "we will continue. Whatever he does, we will continue."

We followed the trail for a short way into the pine grove, until we came to the fire. A man stood up and spoke a word of greeting, which Nehana answered.

"You travel late," the man said softly.

His eyes shone in the firelight. He glanced at each of us, at the three horses and their silver bits.

"We have a long way to go," Nehana answered.

"You have good horses," the man said, still speaking softly. "They can take you far and at a good pace." He rubbed his forehead. "The horses I have seen before. One belongs to Don Roberto. The small one to Señor Gomez. The third I am not sure about, though I think it was ridden by Francisco Roa."

The man stirred the fire so that it shone brighter. He walked over to the horse Nehana was riding and looked closely at its bridle.

"So I thought," he said. "The initial *R. R.* for Roa."

Nehana backed her horse away from the man, but he reached out and grasped hold of the bit.

"What shall I say to those who come this way?" he asked. "To Señor Gomez and Don Roberto and Francisco Roa? They will wish to know where their horses have gone."

"Say what pleases you," Nehana told him, glancing at me and making a motion with her head.

Running Bird and I picked up our reins, ready to flee.

"If you go south," the man said, "I can tell them that you have gone to the north, to the east, to the west. It is simple. All I ask in return is a bridle and a bit. They are for my poor burro who has neither."

"I cannot ride this horse without a bit," Nehana said.

She said no more, but spurred her horse, throwing the man aside into the grass. She circled the fire and we followed her down the woodcutter's trail, leaving the man behind us shouting.

Near dawn we left the pine grove for country

which was open and slanted toward the rising sun. Nehana gave her horse a nudge with her bare heels. We did the same and the horses broke into a trot. Neither Running Bird nor I knew how to ride a horse, but we had learned a little from our journey with the Spaniards and during the long night just past.

Soon we came to a slow-running stream where we watered the horses. As they drank and began to crop the grass along the bank, I kept looking back at the pine grove and the hill beyond, fearful that I would see the Spaniards.

"They have found our trail now that the sun is up," Nehana said, "They will ride faster than we did, having the daylight to go by. Yet they cannot reach this place before the sun is overhead."

She spread a blanket on the grass, as if we were at a fiesta, and laid out some corncakes for us to eat. Running Bird and I were not hungry, so Nehana ate all the cakes. Then she fell asleep. We walked up and down, listening to her breathe, listening for the sound of hoofs, watching the trail we had come along.

Nehana did not move. She lay on her back with her lips half-parted, breathing peacefully.

"Let us take our horses and go," Running Bird said.

"We would not go far," I said. "We are lost without her."

"The Spaniards will find us here," Running Bird said.

The sound of a blue jay fluttering into a tree

made me jump. The stream sounded like men's voices speaking. Then I saw five figures on the hill beyond the pine grove. They were deer coming down to drink at the stream, but I shouted anyway. At my cry Nehana jumped to her feet. She looked in the direction I pointed.

"Deer," she said scornfully.

But she did not lie down again. She got on her horse and we followed her. The stream had a sandy bottom and we rode along between its banks.

"They will follow our tracks to the stream," Nehana said. "They will decide that we rode north, for that is the shortest way."

We rode until midmorning, never leaving the stream. The current washed away all signs of our passage. We came to a wide meadow and Nehana led us across it, and, doubling back, we climbed a high ridge. Near the crest where a few trees grew she stopped and got off her horse, motioning us to follow. We crawled through the brush and rocks until we came to the highest part of the ridge.

Below us lay the country we had traveled that morning—the stream winding northward, the clump of budding cottonwoods where we had watered the horses and Nehana had gone to sleep. Near noon, as we crouched among the trees, three horsemen rode down the hill where I had seen the deer.

The sun glinted on their silver bridles. They rode back and got down from their horses and stood around for a while under the cottonwoods.

Then they jumped into their saddles and started off at a quick trot, two on one side of the stream and one on the other, not in the direction Nehana had said they would ride but down the stream, toward us.

"We go," Nehana said. "We go fast and for our lives."

We crawled back to our horses. Keeping below the crest of the ridge, we rode its length through heavy brush. We rode down into a wide canyon and headed north, back in the direction of the cottonwood grove. We rode fast. We knew that the Spaniards would find our tracks where we had left the stream and crossed the meadow and climbed the ridge.

11

Night was falling as we again reached the stream and the grove of budding cottonwoods. We had seen no sign of the Spaniards during the afternoon, but they were not far behind us.

Our horses had begun to stumble, so we watered them and went a short way and rode into a draw that was hidden from the stream.

"We will rest here until the moon rises," Nehana said. "It is too dark now for the Spaniards to see our tracks. Lie down and sleep. I will keep watch."

Running Bird and I bathed our faces in the stream and ate some of the tortillas she had brought. Then we went back where the horses were tied and laid down. I slept for a while and had a bad dream and awoke to the sound of my black dog barking.

He was standing beside me in the grass, faced toward the stream. Running Bird was already on her feet trying to quiet him. I reached out and put my hand over his muzzle, but he squirmed away and kept barking. I ran toward the horses, which Nehana had untied.

"He may be barking at a wild animal," I said.

"It is time to go," Nehana said.

The moon was rising over the hill behind us. But it was dark night in the draw where we were hidden. There was no other way out of the draw save the narrow way we had come. We started toward the stream where the moonlight glittered on the water and the cottonwoods. My black dog was still barking.

Nehana said, "I would rather die than be captured again."

I felt the same as Nehana did. I followed her closely and Running Bird followed me. The three of us rode out of the draw, gripping the horses' reins. We were ready to flee at the first sight of the Spaniards.

Before we reached the stream, two horsemen came out of the trees into the moonlight. Something about them—the size of their horses and the way they rode—made me think they were Indians. We were not more than a dozen paces apart. Still I was not certain.

The black dog rushed at them and stopped. Then one of the horsemen shouted to us, a single word in Navaho. I knew the voice. I would know it anywhere. Quietly I answered him.

I think Tall Boy was more surprised than I was, for he rode up slowly and sat there on his horse staring at me. Mando, his friend, also stared at me.

Nehana said, "The Spaniards are near."

Without a word the five of us rode off, Tall Boy taking the lead. We rode hard until the first light of day. Tall Boy spoke only once to me during the long night. It was about my black dog and I have forgotten what he said, but I remember that it made me happy.

Near dawn while we slept, the Spaniards came along the stream. My black dog barked when they were still a distance away. We mounted our horses and rode out of the ravine where we were hidden. Mist was rising from the water. A cool wind blew from the east. It brought to us the sound of hoof-beats and the neigh of a horse.

"We cannot outride the Spaniards," Tall Boy said. "We will therefore go slowly on the trail toward home, as if we did not fear them. We will not heed them unless they speak. We will not fight unless they attack us."

Tall Boy said this solemnly but I knew by the fire deep in his eyes that he wanted to kill all the Spaniards, that he would do so if the chance came.

We went in single file along a bank of the stream, toward the rising sun. The sound of hoofs was muffled in the tall grass. Mando and Tall Boy rode last with their lances sheathed and their bows unstrung.

As the sun came up the three Spaniards over-took us. The one with the white teeth spoke to Tall Boy.

"The women ride horses that belong to us," he said in Navaho. "The horses were stolen."

Tall Boy did not answer. He spurred his horse

and trotted up beside Nehana and me, saying in a whisper that we should not dismount. We rode on, bunched together, the Spaniards close behind us. There was no sound except the ringing of hawk's bells on their silver bits.

We came to a clump of trees beside the stream. Here the leader shouted at us. I saw him swing down from the saddle and take a rifle from its holster. The two other Spaniards pulled up their horses.

Tall Boy told us to ride on and stop behind the trees. Then he said something to Mando under his breath. Together they gave a piercing war cry.

I had heard this cry before, many times since my childhood. It always froze my blood to hear it, and it did now. It sounded to me as if some evil spirit had leaped out from the far depths of the earth. The cry was not a human sound nor the sound that any animal makes whether in pain or fright.

The leader held the rifle in one hand and the reins of his stallion. At the sound of the war cries the horse leaped sidewise, dragging his master with him. By the time the Spaniard loosed the reins and brought the rifle to his shoulder, Tall Boy swept past him and in one swift thrust planted the long lance.

The other Spaniards, seeing the death of their leader, fled into the trees. Tall Boy and Mando did not pursue them. Instead, they motioned to us and set off up the stream. There was no sign of the two men.

We had not gone far when a shot sounded from the trees where the Spaniards were hidden. A second shot struck Tall Boy.

He clutched the saddle horn but made no sound. He spurred his horse into a gallop and we followed. There were no more shots. The Spaniards did not come out of the trees. In a short time Tall Boy slowed his horse. He had turned pale and blood showed on his back.

He stopped his horse and said, "I can no longer sit in the saddle. Take this rope and tie me there."

Mando and I took the rope and put it around his waist and tied him so that he could lean over the neck of the horse.

The Spaniards did not follow us. We went slowly up the stream the way Tall Boy and Mando had come. We traveled slowly all day. At dusk we made camp and helped Tall Boy down from his horse and laid him on the grass. He ate a little food and drank some water, but I feared that he was dying. I sat beside him through the night, bringing him water when he asked for it. I prayed that he would not die.

Tall Boy seemed better the next day, so we rode faster and longer, making many leagues. But on the third day he could not climb into the saddle.

Out of two willow poles and a blanket we fashioned a sled and put him on it, hitching the sled to the strongest horse.

We went slowly that day and the next and on

the fifth morning, as the sun rose, we came within sight of our canyon.

"You are near home," I said to Tall Boy. "Soon you will be well."

Tall Boy looked at me and tried to smile.

"I will ride on," I said, "and tell the medicine man."

"Yes," said Tall Boy, "tell him that he is needed."

12

I rode hard toward home. The stone cliffs were dark, but far above them the early light lay on their crests and the trees that grew there shone as if they were on fire.

A dawn wind blew, smelling of earth and wood smoke and corn ripe in the fields. It was a Navaho wind. Joyously I breathed it in.

White Deer was tending her flock by the river. She must have believed me dead long ago. For a moment I thought she would flee. I spoke to her and rode on and only then did she run after me, asking many questions all at once.

It was the same with my mother and father and sister. They came running out of the hogan and stood there gazing at me as though I were a spirit. Not until I spoke and told them that Tall Boy was wounded did they move or say anything.

Bitter Water, the medicine man, was in the next village. My father and four other men went out to meet Tall Boy and bring him in. When they came back, carrying him on a litter, the medicine man had come with his bag of curing things—two round blue stones, a small object with an oval knot in it that looked like an eye, one eagle feather and a groaning stick, a piece of wood from a lightning-struck tree.

Tall Boy was laid in the grass under a big sycamore, close beside the river. He was pale and gaunt-faced and kept his eyes closed, even when I spoke to him. The medicine man cleaned the wide wound in his shoulder with river water and the juice of mottled berries. Then he touched him all over from head to foot, gently with the blue stones, and at last with the little object that looked like an eye.

That night Tall Boy ate something and the next day his father came and moved him to their hogan, not far up the river. My sister helped me cook food that I thought he would like and we took it to him. We went every day and after a week he began to sit up. The color came back to his face, but he could not use his right arm. It hung limp at his side. My sister said that he would never use that arm again.

She said this to me as we were riding home. She said nothing more, but I knew what she meant. She wanted me to understand that he would never be able to hunt again, nor go out on raids with the other warriors.

The next morning my mother said, "You have thirty sheep and they all need shearing. But before they are shorn there are beans and squash to plant."

"I will start tomorrow," I said. "This morning I want to cook deer meat. Tall Boy likes it better than anything else."

My mother was combing her hair. She stopped

and looked at me. "There are many women who can cook deer meat for Tall Boy. The moon is right for planting."

"The moon will be right tomorrow," I said.

My mother went on combining her hair. "Your sister has told me that he has an arm that will never again pull a bowstring or throw a lance. This is bad fortune. He will no longer be a warrior nor a hunter. He will have to sit with the women. Perhaps he will learn to weave and cut wood and shear sheep."

My friend Running Bird said, "I feel sorry for him."

Nehana, who was going to marry the son of a chief of a village far up the river, said the same.

My mother tied her hair and stood up, pointing to the bag of squash seeds hanging by the door. "Plant the seeds deep," she said, "for the earth is very dry."

Walking along in the hot sun, with the bag heavy on my shoulder, I made deep holes with a stick and dropped the seeds in, three seeds in each hole. But my thoughts were not there in the field. Even when I tried thinking of my sheep, I was unhappy.

I did not care, not for myself, whether Tall Boy would ever be able to hunt again or ride with the warriors. But my sister and my mother did care and there was nothing they would not do to keep me from marrying a cripple. It was my father who would decide and he had said nothing. Yet this did not give me any comfort, for he usually did what they wanted him to do.

When the squash and beans were planted, I helped with the shearing and drove my flock to pastures by the river. The grass was not so good as it was on the mesa, but we were afraid to go too far from the village. Every week my mother and I went to visit Tall Boy and his family. She never again said anything about his arm and when he had trouble, when it was awkward for him to do something, she always looked away in pity.

By the time the hot days came we did not go to see Tall Boy anymore. Once in a while he rode down to see us, but he did not stay long or have much to say. Then other boys began to visit. They came and sat under the trees in front of our hogan and joked with each other and played stick games.

One night my mother said, "It is time for the girl to become a woman. Tomorrow I will send word of the Womanhood Ceremony."

13

On the first day of Kin-nadl-dah, twenty-one relatives and many friends came to our hogan, also Bitter Water, the medicine man, and his singers. My mother dressed me in my best tunic and gave me all her turquoise and silver jewelry to wear. She combed my hair so that it fell loose around my shoulders and tied it in the middle with a string of sacred buckskin.

Everyone told me how handsome I looked. My aunt, who was very old and never had been married, said that I was too pretty for any man she had ever seen. I walked back and forth in front of the hogan, so all my relatives and friends could look at me.

I walked there for only a short time, because my mother brought four sacks of corn from the storehouse and led me to the big grinding stone.

"The Womanhood Ceremony lasts four days," she said, "so we need lots of flour to eat. You are not good at the grinding stone, but now you must put your mind to it and make four full sacks of fine meal."

In my best clothes and my borrowed jewelry, I knelt and began to grind the corn. I worked for only a short time.

My cousin came to me and said, "Wood is scarce."

I laid my grinding tool aside and went to the bottom of the orchard and chopped an armload of wood and stacked it in front of the fire. Then I began grinding corn again. After a while, one of the neighbors handed me an empty jar.

"Your mother tells me," she said, "that goat's milk is needed."

I jumped up and ran down to the river and found a goat and milked it and brought the jar back. Again I began to grind the corn.

Then my uncle came. "Your aunt wishes a blanket," he said.

It went on in such a fashion all that day. Everyone wanted something. Everyone gave me orders. I was flying here and there and between times I knelt at the grinding stone. This was to make me industrious and obedient, my mother said.

During these four days, early each morning I had to run east, south, west, and north, as though I was running a race. This was to make me a good runner. Furthermore, I could not eat sweet things nor anything with salt in it, nor drink too much water. Nor was I allowed to scratch myself. And I was told to sleep as little as possible. These things were to make me comely.

The fourth morning men relatives dug a large hole in front of the hogan and kept a fire burning there all day. Toward evening when the fire died down, the women lined the hole with corn husks and poured in a lot of mush, covering it over with more husks.

At nightfall we ate some of the corncake and went into the hogan and I sat on the west side across from the door. Then the medicine man sang the twelve songs. The other singers chanted lucky songs about sheep and jewelry and soft goods. They chanted all night. I had to keep awake and listen or else I would have bad luck.

Just before dawn my mother gave me a basket with water and yucca root in it and helped me to wash my hair. Then, as the sun came up, I ran out from the hogan toward the east, past the orchard and the cornfield.

All the boys ran after me, even Tall Boy, who still had not gained his strength. We raced to the river and back again. But it was not a real race to see who could run the fastest. For if any of the boys had won, had beaten me by so much as a step, then they would become old and toothless long before I did.

I had hoped that Tall Boy would not try to run at all. But he was the first to start after me. I ran much slower than I could, hoping that it would help him. This he did not like. He shouted at me to go faster.

"You run like an old woman," he cried.

I went a little faster and came to the river and floundered around, pretending to slip on the grass bank.

"My grandmother runs faster than you," he said.

His words made me angry and I began to run as fast as I could and left him far behind. Pale and out of breath, he came in last. The rest of the morning he went around scowling. I tried to make him smile but he would not forgive me for running fast, even though he had taunted me.

"You do not need to feel sorry about my arm," he said. "It is getting stronger every day."

"Soon you will be bending a bow," I answered.

"You do not think so, but I will bend many bows before I die," he said.

"I think so."

"No one thinks so, but I will," he said.

That afternoon when the relatives and friends and the medicine man and his singers had gone, my mother sent me to the field. She gave me a sack of pinto beans and a long pointed stick. Though I was now a woman, I had to work the rest of the day planting seeds.

Tall Boy rode through the field on his way home, but did not stop.

"You think that I went to the white man's village just to rescue you," he said as he passed. "You are wrong. I went there for another reason."

I watched him ride away, sitting stooped in the saddle, one shoulder lower than the other, and my heart went out to him.

14

The pinto beans pushed up through the earth and the peaches began to swell. Wool from the shearing was stored away for winter weaving. My father and brother went into the mountains and brought back deer meat which we cut into strips and dried. It was a good summer and a good autumn.

Then early one winter morning three Long Knives came. They were from the white man's fort and they brought a message from their chief. When all of our people were gathered in the meadow one of the soldiers read the message, using Navaho words. He read fast and did not speak clearly, but this is what I remember.

> People of the Navaho Tribe are commanded to take their goods and leave Canyon de Chelly.

The Long Knife read more from the paper which I do not remember. Then he fastened the paper to a tree where all in the village could see it and the three soldiers rode away.

There was silence after the soldiers left. Everyone was too stunned to speak or move. We had been threatened before by the Long Knives, but we lived at peace in our canyon, so why should they wish to harm us?

Everyone stared at the yellow paper fastened to the cottonwood tree, as if it were alive and had some evil power. Then, after a long time, Tall Boy walked to the tree. Grasping the paper, he tore it into many pieces and threw them into the river. We watched the pieces float away, thinking as they disappeared that so had the threat of the white men. But we were wrong. At night, in the dark of the moon, the Long Knives came.

The morning of that day we knew they were coming. Little Beaver, who was tending his mother's sheep, saw them from the high mesa. He left his flock and ran across the mesa and down the trail, never stopping.

He fell in front of his mother's hogan and lay there like a stone until someone threw a gourd of water in his face. By that time all the people in the village stood waiting for him to speak. He jumped to his feet and pointed into the south.

"The white men come," he cried. "The sun glints on their knives. They are near."

"How many?" Tall Boy said.

"Many," cried Little Beaver, "too many."

My father said, "We will take our goods and go into the high country. We will return when they are gone."

"We will go," said other men.

But Tall Boy held up his hand and shouted, facing the elder Indians, "If we flee they will follow. If we flee, our goods will remain to be captured. It is better to stay and fight the Long Knives."

"It is not wise to fight," my father said.

"No, it is not," my uncle said, and all the older men repeated what he said.

It was decided then that we should go. But Tall Boy still would not yield. He called to five of the young men to join him in the fight. They went and stood by him.

"We will need you," my father said to the six young men, "We will have to go into high country. Your strength will help us there."

Tall Boy was unbending. My father looked at him, at his arm held helplessly at his side.

"How is it, Tall Boy, that you will fight?" he said. "You cannot string a bow or send a lance. Tell me, I am listening."

I watched Tall Boy's face darken.

"If you stay and cannot fight, what will happen?" my father asked him. "You will be killed. Others will be killed."

Tall Boy said nothing. It hurt me to watch his face as he listened to words that he knew were true. I left them talking and went down to the river. When I came back Tall Boy had gathered his band of warriors and gone.

We began to pack at once. Each family took what it could carry. There were five horses in the village and they were driven up the mesa trail and left there. The sheep and goats were driven a league away into a secret canyon where they could graze. My flock, my thirty sheep, went too, with the rest. I would have gone with them if I had not thought that in a few days the Long Knives would leave and we could come back to our village. I would never have abandoned them.

When the sun was high we filed out of the village and followed the river north, walking through the shallow water. At dusk we reached the trail that led upward to the south mesa. Before we went up the trail the jars were filled with water. We took enough to last us for a week and five sheep to slaughter. The cornmeal we carried would last that long. By that time the soldiers would be gone.

The soldiers could not follow our path from the village because the flowing water covered our footsteps as fast as they were made. But when we moved out of the river our steps showed clear in the sand. After we were all on the trail some of the men broke branches from a tree and went back and swept away the marks we had left. There was no sign for the soldiers to see. They could not tell whether we had gone up the river or down.

The trail was narrow and steep. It was mostly slabs of stone which we scrambled over, lifting ourselves from one to the other. We crawled as much as we walked. In places the sheep had to be carried and two of them slipped and fell into a ravine. The trail upward was less than half a mile long, but night was falling before we reached the end.

We made camp on the rim of the mesa, among rocks and stunted piñon trees. We did not think that the soldiers would come until morning, but we lighted no fires and ate a cold supper of corncakes. The moon rose and in a short time shone down into the canyon. It showed the river winding toward the south, past our peach orchards and corrals and hogans. Where the tall cliffs ended, where the river wound out of the canyon into the flatlands, the moon shone on white tents and tethered horses.

"The soldiers have come," my uncle said. "They will not look for us until morning. Lie down and sleep."

We made our beds among the rocks but few of us slept. At dawn we did not light fires, for fear the soldiers would see the rising smoke, and ate a cold breakfast. My father ordered everyone to gather stones and pile them where the trail entered the mesa. He posted a guard of young men at the trail head to use the stones if the soldiers came to attack us. He then sent three of the fastest runners to keep watch on the army below.

I was one of the three sent. We crawled south along the rim of the mesa and hid among the rocks, within sight of each other. From where I crouched behind a piñon tree, I had a clear view of the soldiers' camp.

As the sun rose and shone down into the narrow canyon I could see the Long Knives watering their horses. They were so far below me that the horses seemed no larger than dogs. Soon afterward six of the soldiers rode northward. They were riding along the banks of the river in search of our tracks. Once they got off their horses and two of them climbed up to Rainbow Cave where cliff dwellers had lived long ago. But they found the houses deserted.

The soldiers went up the river, past the trail that led to the place where we were hidden. They did not return until the sun was low. As they rode slowly along, they scanned the cliff that soared above them, their eyes sweeping the rocks and trees, but they did not halt. They rode down the river to their tents and unsaddled the horses. We watched until they lighted their supper fires, then we went back to our camp.

Tall Boy was sitting on a rock near the top of the trail, at work on a lance. He held the shaft between his knees, using his teeth and a hand to wrap it with a split reed.

I was surprised to see him sitting there, for he and the other young warriors had ridden out of the canyon on the morning the Long Knives came. No one had heard from them since that day. Even his mother and father and sisters, who were hiding with us on the mesa, did not know where he was. At first I thought that he had changed his mind and come back to help protect them. But this was not the reason for his return.

Mumbling something that I could not understand, he went on with his work. I stood above him and as I looked down I noticed a deep scratch across his forehead and that a loop of his braided hair had pulled loose.

"Did you hurt yourself climbing the trail?" I said.

He knotted the reed around the shaft and bit the ends off with his teeth. His right arm hung useless at his side.

"The climb is not difficult," he said.

It was a very difficult climb, but I did not say so, since he wanted me to think otherwise. "Where are the warriors?" I asked him. "Are they coming to help us?"

"They have left the canyon," he said.

"But you did not go," I said, noticing now that he had lost one of his moccasins.

For an instant he glanced up at me. In his eyes I saw a look of shame, or was it anger? I saw that the young warriors had left him behind with the women and old men and children. He was no longer of any use to them.

He held up the lance and sighted along the shaft. "It has an iron point," he said. "I found it in the west country."

"It will be a mighty weapon against the Long Knives," I said.

"It is a weapon that does not require two hands."

"One hand or the other," I said, "it does not matter."

That night we ate another cold supper, yet everyone was in good spirits. The white soldiers had searched the canyon and found no trace of us. We felt secure. We felt that in the morning they would ride away, leaving us in peace.

15

In the morning guards were set again at the head of the trail. Running Bird and I crawled to our places near the piñon tree and crouched there as the sun rose and shone down on the camp of the Long Knives. Other lookouts hid themselves along the rim of the mesa, among the rocks and brush.

Nothing had changed in the night. There were the same number of tents among the trees and the same number of horses tethered on the riverbank. Our hogans were deserted. No smoke rose from the ovens or the fire pits. There was no sound of sheep bells.

The camp of the Long Knives was quiet until the sun was halfway up the morning sky. Men strolled about as if they had nothing to do. Two were even fishing in the river with long willow poles. Then—while Running Bird and I watched a squirrel in the piñon tree, trying to coax him down with a nut—I saw from the corner of an eye a puff of smoke rise slowly from our village. It seemed no larger than my hand. A second puff rose in the windless air and a third.

"Our homes are burning!"

The word came from the lookout who was far out on the mesa rim, closest to the village. It was passed from one lookout to the other, at last to me, and I ran with it back to our camp and told the news to my father.

"We will build new homes," he said. "When the Long Knives leave we will go into the forest and cut timber. We will build hogans that are better than those the soldiers burned."

"Yes," people said when they heard the news, "we will build a new village."

Tall Boy said nothing. He sat working on his lance, using his teeth and one hand, and did not look up.

I went back to the piñon and my father went with me. All our homes had burned to the ground. Only gray ashes and a mound of earth marked the place where each had stood. The Long Knives were sitting under a tree eating, and their horses cropped the meadow grass.

My father said, "They will ride away now that they have destroyed our village."

But they did not ride away. While we watched, ten soldiers with hatchets went into our peach orchard, which still held its summer leaves. Their blades glinted in the sunlight. Their voices drifted up to us where we were huddled among the rocks.

Swinging the hatchets as they sang, the soldiers began to cut the limbs from the peach trees. The blows echoed through the canyon. They did not stop until every branch lay on the ground and only bare stumps, which looked like a line of scarecrows, were left.

Then, at the last, the Long Knives stripped all the bark from the stumps, so that we would not have this to eat when we were starving.

"Now they will go," my father said, "and leave us in peace."

But the soldiers laid their axes aside. They spurred their horses into a gallop and rode through the cornfield, trampling the green corn. Then they rode through the field of ripening beans and the melon patch, until the fields were no longer green but the color of the red earth.

"We will plant more melons and corn and beans," my father said.

"There are no seeds left," I said. "And if we had seeds and planted them they would not bear before next summer."

We watched while the soldiers rode back to their camp. We waited for them to fold their tents and leave. All that day and the next we watched from the rim of the mesa. On the third day the soldiers cut alder poles and made a large lean-to, which they roofed over with the branches. They also dug a fire pit and started to build an oven of mud and stones.

It was then we knew that the Long Knives did not plan to leave the canyon.

"They have learned that we are camped here," my father said. "They do not want to climb the cliff and attack us. It is easier to wait there by the river until we starve."

16

Clouds blew up next morning and it began to rain. We cut brush and limbs from the piñon pines and made shelters. That night, after the rain stopped, we went to the far side of the mesa where our fires could not be seen by the soldiers and cooked supper. Though there was little danger that the soldiers would attack us, my father set guards to watch the trail.

We were very careful with our jars of water, but on the sixth day the jars were empty. That night my father sent three of us down the trail to fill the jars at the river. We left soon after dark. There was no moon to see by so we were a long time getting to the river. When we started back up the trail we covered our tracks as carefully as we could. But the next day the soldiers found that we had been there. After that there were always two soldiers at the bottom of the trail, at night and during the day.

The water we carried back lasted longer than the first. When the jars were nearly empty it rained hard for two days and we caught water in our blankets and stored it. We also discovered a deep stone crevice filled with rainwater, enough for the rest of the summer. But the food we had brought with us, though we ate only half as much as we did when we were home in the village, ran low. We ate all of the corn and slaughtered the sheep we had brought. Then we ground up the sheep bones and made a broth, which was hard to swallow. We lived on this for two days and when it was gone we had nothing to eat.

Old Bear, who had been sick since we came to the mesa, died on the third day. And that night the baby of Shining Tree died. The next night was the first night of the full moon. It was then that my father said that we must leave.

Dawn was breaking high over the mesa when we reached the bottom of the trail. There was no sign of the soldiers.

My father led us northward through the trees, away from our old village and the soldiers' camp. It would have been wiser if we had traveled in the riverbed, but there were many who were so weak they could not walk against the current.

As soon as it grew light we found patches of wild berries among the trees and ate them while we walked. The berries were ripe and sweet and gave us strength. We walked until the sun was overhead; then, because four of the women could go no farther, we stopped and rested in a cave.

We gathered more berries and some roots and stayed there until the moon came up. Then we started off again, following the river northward, traveling by the moon's white glow. When it swung westward and left the canyon in darkness we lay down among the trees. We had gone no more than two leagues in a day and part of a night, but we were hopeful that the soldiers would not follow us.

In the morning we built a small fire and roasted a basket of roots. Afterward the men held council to decide whether to go on or to stay where we were camped.

"They have burned our homes," my father said. "They have cut down the trees of our orchard. They have trampled our gardens into the earth. What else can the soldiers do to us that they have not already done?"

"The Long Knives can drive us out of the canyon," my uncle said, "and leave us to walk the wilderness."

At last it was decided that we stay.

We set about the cutting of brush and poles to make shelters. About mid-morning, while we were still working on the lean-tos, the sound of hoofs striking stone came from the direction of the river.

Taking up his lance, Tall Boy stepped behind a tree. The rest of us stood in silence. Even the children were silent. We were like animals who hear the hunter approach but from terror cannot flee.

The Long Knives came out of the trees in single file. They were joking among themselves and at first did not see us. The leader was a young man with a red cloth knotted around his neck. He was looking back, talking to someone, as he came near the place where Tall Boy stood hidden.

Tall Boy stepped from behind the tree, squarely in his path. Still the leader did not see him.

Raising the lance, Tall Boy quickly took aim and drew back, ready to send it toward the leader of the Long Knives. He had practiced with the lance before we came down the mesa, time after time during all of one day, trying to get used to throwing it with his left hand. With his right hand he had been the best of all the warriors. It was with a lance that he had killed the brown bear beyond Rainbow Mountain, a feat of great skill.

But now, as the iron-tipped weapon sped from his grasp, it did not fly straight. It wobbled and then curved upward, struck the branch of a tree, and fell broken at the feet of the soldier's horse.

The horse suddenly stopped, tossing its head. Only then did the soldier turn to see the broken lance lying in front of him. He looked around, searching for the enemy who had thrown it. He looked at my father, at my uncle, at me. His eyes swept the small open space where he stood, the women the children, the old people, all of us still too frightened to move or speak.

Tall Boy, as soon as he had thrown the lance, dodged behind the tree where he had hidden before, backed away into the brush and quietly disappeared. I saw his face as he went past me. He no longer looked like a warrior. He looked like a boy, crushed and beaten, who flees for his life.

The rest of the Long Knives rode up and surrounded us. They searched us one by one, making certain that no one carried a weapon, then they headed us down the canyon.

We passed the ruined fields of beans and corn and melons, the peach trees stripped of their bark and branches, our burned-out homes. We turned our eyes away from them and set our faces. Our tears were unshed.

Soon we were to learn that others bore the same fate, that the whole nation of the Navahos was on the march. With the Long Knives at their backs, the clans were moving—the Bitter-Water, Under-His-Cover, Red-House, Trail-to-the-Garden, Standing-House, Red-Forehead, Poles-Strung-Out—all the Navahos were marching into captivity.

17

The sky was gray and the air smelled of bitter winds. The Long Knives drove us along the river and through the portals of the canyon. Like sheep before the shepherd, we went without a sound.

By noon on that day snow fell out of the gray sky. A sharp wind blew against us. The Long Knives made camp in a wooded draw and told us to do likewise. We stayed there in the draw until the snow stopped, until two days had gone. Then on the third morning we set off again.

My father asked one of the Long Knives where they were taking us. The soldier said, "Fort Sumner." He pointed southward and that was all.

On that day we met Navahos from Blue Water Canyon, more than fifty of them. They came down from their village, driven by the Long Knives. Their clothes were ragged and all were on foot. Most of them were old men and women, but one girl about my age was carrying two young children on her back. They were heavy for her and I asked if I could help her carry one of them.

The girl's name was Little Rainbow. She was

small but pretty like a flower and her children, a boy and a girl, looked like flowers too, with their round faces and big dark eyes. She gave me the girl and I made a sling and carried her on my back the rest of that day.

Toward evening we came upon another band of Navahos. There were about a hundred of them, a few on horses. They belonged to the Coyote Clan and had been on the trail for a week, prodded along by five soldiers.

We lighted fires that night and had a gathering. The Long Knives left us alone, but we could see them watching us from the trees while we chanted our songs and our prayers. Little Rainbow came and we sat together in the grass, playing with the children. She took the girl with her when she went off to sleep, but in the morning gave her back to me.

Sometime in the night, Tall Boy slipped into our camp and lay down by the fire. We found him there in the morning, his clothes torn and his feet bare and bleeding. He ate the mush I brought to him but would not talk. He had the same shamed look about him that I had seen when he fled from the Long Knives, his lance lying broken upon the ground.

The trail led south and eastward across rough country and we went slowly because of the old people. We had two wagons with good horses but they were not enough to carry all those who needed help. We made scarcely a league during the whole morning.

At noon two large bands of Navahos overtook us. They were mostly men, some of them wounded in a fight with the Long Knives. They went by us with their eyes on the ground, silent and weaponless.

That afternoon we saw many bands of Navahos. They came from all directions, from the high country and from the valleys. It was like a storm when water trickles from everywhere and flows into the river and the river flows full. This was the way the trail looked as night fell, like a dark-flowing river.

Little Rainbow did not come for her child when we camped that night and I asked my mother what I should do.

"There is nothing to do," she said.

My sister said, "You were foolish to take the child. You have enough to carry without her."

"We will find the girl tomorrow," my mother said, "or she will find us. In the meantime she knows that her child is safe."

We did not find her the next day. Tall Boy went out looking at sunrise, but soon returned, saying that a soldier had threatened him. The soldier told him to go back to his clan and not to wander around or someone would shoot him.

All day as we trudged eastward I looked for Little Rainbow. I asked people I did not know if they had seen her. Everyone shook their heads. In a way I was glad that I did not find her. I was carrying three rolled-up blankets and a jar filled with cornmeal. It was a heavy burden even without the little girl. But she was good all the time, making happy sounds as the two of us went along.

As on the day before, Navahos by the hundreds came out of the mountains and forests to join us.

The river flowed slower now and many old people began to falter. At first, the Long Knives rode back and forth, urging them on if they lay down beside the trail. But so many fell that afternoon when the cold wind blew from the north that the soldiers did not take notice anymore, except to jeer at them.

The march went on until dusk. Fires were lighted and people gathered around them. Our clan said little to each other. We were unhappy and afraid, not knowing where we were driven.

"The soldiers tell me that it is a place of running water and deep grass," my father said. "But it lies a long walk to the east."

He said this every night as we huddled around the fire. I think he believed it. He wanted us to believe it, too.

"Cast your eyes around," he said. "You will see many people sitting beside their fires. They are hungry but not starving. They are cold but they do not freeze. They are unhappy. Yet they are alive."

"We are walking to our deaths," my mother said. "The old die now. The young die later. But we all die."

Tall Boy stared at the fire, saying nothing. He had said little since that day when he tried to throw his iron-tipped lance and had failed. The Navahos, his people, were captives of the Long Knives and there was nothing he could do to free them. Once he had been haughty, his wide shoulders held straight, his black eyes looking coldly at everyone. I wished, as I sat there beside him, that he would act haughty once more.

My sister took the little girl from my lap, where she was sleeping. "She is heavy," Lapana said.

"No wonder," my mother answered. "She eats a lot, as much as I do almost. And food is scarce. Every day there will be less until there is none."

I took the child back and wrapped her in a blanket and lay down with her in my arms.

The fire died away and I could see the stars. I wondered what the little girl's name was. She was like a flower, like a flower in a spring meadow. I gave her that name—Meadow Flower—as she lay beside me.

The north wind was cold and far off among the trees the horses of the Long Knives were restless.

18

A new moon showed in the west and grew full and waned and still we moved on.

The hills and the piñon country fell behind. There were few streams anymore. When we came to water we drank deeply and filled our jars to the brim. The land was covered with gray brush and rolled away so far that it hurt the eyes to look.

By this time there were thousands of Navahos on the march. We spread out along the trail for miles, each clan keeping to itself, by command of the soldiers, who rode at the head of the column and at the rear. At night the Long Knives posted guards near all the Indian fires.

We now had six wagons, each drawn by two horses. At first they carried only water and flour and blankets, but as old people grew lame or sick the supplies were taken out of the wagons to make room for them.

For those who died, we scooped out shallow holes in the frozen earth and laid them there, putting rocks on the graves to keep the wild animals away.

My grandmother was the second old woman to die. Somehow she got herself out of the wagon where she had been riding and stumbled off into the brush. She lay down and pulled a blanket over her head. She wanted to die and drove us away when we tried to help her.

Food grew scarce. The soldiers sent some of the young Navahos out to kill deer and buffalo, but hunting was not good.

People began to eat their pets and from then on I never let my black dog out of sight. Before I went to sleep at night I put a leather rope around his neck and tied it to my wrist, as I had at the crone's hut.

In the beginning I fed the little girl first, which did not please my mother or my sister. When food ran low I fed her from my share so they could not complain. My back got very sore from the sling I carried her in. Tall Boy fashioned a carrying board from brush and pieces of cloth. This made my load seem lighter.

The country changed during the next moon. The flatlands rolled up into hills and we crossed many draws where water ran. Grass was springing everywhere, which helped us feed our starving horses. Every afternoon rain fell and our clothes never dried out from one day to the next.

It was about this time that the little girl became ill. We had a chant for her one night. Then the medicine man went over her from head to foot with his gentle hands. He drove away some of the evil spirits so that she smiled and was better.

A large band of Navahos came straggling down upon us. They were ragged and hungry and many were sick. Many, they said, had died on the trail. They came from the rim rock country far to the west. Now the line of people struggling along stretched from one horizon to the other. In the daytime flocks of buzzards followed us and at dusk coyotes sat on the hills and howled.

Spring came overnight, with fleecy clouds and larks soaring from the grass. It made us happy to know that winter was behind us. Then there was word that we were only two suns' march from the end of the trail, from a place near Fort Sumner.

The place was called Bosque Redondo and we reached it at noon of the third day. It was in a bend of a big looping river, flat bottomland covered with brush.

We were on a small rise when we looked down upon it first. My mother had not cried since we left our canyon. But she cried now as she stood there and looked down upon this gray country that was to be our home.

I planned to go out in search of the little girl's mother the next morning after we reached Bosque Redondo. But the child woke me before dawn with her cries, so I minded her all day and sent Running Bird to look for her mother. She came back about dark, not having found her. That night the medicine man came and touched the little girl and we had a sing.

The night was half over and I was sitting beside the fire with the little girl in my arms. She held one of my fingers tight in her small fist and I was singing a song to her about a bird in a pine tree. I sang another song to her and another before I was aware that she was no longer listening, that she had died quietly in my arms.

In the morning I went out to search for her mother. I went to hundreds of lean-tos and fires and when night came I lay down in the brush and went to sleep, wondering what I could say when I found her.

In the morning I started out again. A young man told me that he had seen the girl I described to him and she was living on the bank of the river near a tree, which he pointed out. It was far away and it took me until noon to make my way through the hundreds of people working to make shelters for themselves.

I saw her before I reached the river and she saw me. We ran toward each other through the thick brush.

There was an open place covered with pale grass and we both stopped as we came to it and looked at each other.

It was a short time that we stood there yet it seemed long. Then I went over to her and put my hand in hers. I could not think of anything to say, but I did not need to. She had been crying and I knew that her other child had died too. We put our arms around each other and stood together in the spring sun without speaking.

19

The gray flatland between the banks of the river was divided among the clans. Everyone shared alike and each family built some sort of a shelter—a cave in the earth, a brush lean-to, or a hut—out of whatever things could be gathered.

Our hut was made of driftwood we found along the river and strips of old canvas. It kept out the sun but not the winds and it was hard to walk around in without bumping your head on something.

Food was soon gone, so the Long Knives passed out parcels of flour to all the families. There were few among us who did not get sick, for the flour was made of wheat, which we were not used to eating. And the water from the muddy river was bitter.

There were several hundred Indians already living at Bosque Redondo. They were Apaches who had been driven out of their country and were being held prisoners by the Long Knives.

The Apaches are smaller than we are, but thick and very strong. They are also quarrelsome. They want their way about everything and if they do not get it they fight. They fought with us as soon as we came, saying that the land belonged to them and that we were stealing it.

My father and two other headmen from the clans told them that the Navahos did not like Bosque Redondo. If the Apaches wanted it they could have it. All we wanted was to live on it until the Long Knives found us a better place. These words did not please the Apaches and they tried to hurt us whenever they could.

When every family had shelter and food the Long Knives sent all the men who were able to work with a hoe to break up the earth and plant it with corn and with wheat, which we did not like. Then they set them to digging ditches to carry water from the river into the fields.

Thus summer began at Bosque Redondo, our new home. My mother and sister and I, like all the other women, had little to do. There was no corn to grind. Wagons came filled with flour. White soldiers stood in it up to their knees and passed it out to us on big wooden shovels. There were no sheep to tend or wool to shear and weave into blankets. There were no hunters to bring in hides to scrape and stretch and make into leggings. We were idle most of the time.

It was the same with Tall Boy. He would come over every morning after breakfast and sit around in front of our hut until the sun was well up. Then he would wander down to the river and lie in the sun some more. He liked to show the other young Navahos the big white scar on his shoulder, where the Spaniard's bullet had struck him. Only he told them it was one of the Long Knives who had given him the scar.

The other men were also idle most of the time, once the fields were planted and the water ditches dug. Like Tall Boy they enjoyed talking about the days before they came to Bosque Redondo. They sat around and bragged about things they had done. They made threats against the Long Knives, but the threats were weak and spoken quietly. They gossiped worse than the women. The heart had gone out of them. The spirit had left their bodies.

It was a bad summer in Bosque Redondo. There were ghosts and witches everywhere and many people sickened and died. Then the first crop failed. There was little rain and our men had trouble leading water up from the river. Some of the fields were planted again, but winds blew the seeds away and fall came without a harvest.

There was much talk after that about the Long Knives who lived in the gray-walled fort in the midst of our fields. Hardly a day went by that some new story did not spread from hut to hut about them. The wheat flour would run out before winter came. The flour was cursed and if we went on eating it we would all die. The Long Knives wanted us to die and so we would, in some way or another.

One story came to use from three different men, who had been in a place fifteen days' journey to the north. Each man brought the same story, so it was surely true. The place was called Sand Creek and it was near a town which was in the mountains. They said that a village of Cheyennes and Arapahos were asleep in their lodges. There was a white preacher and he rode out from the town with some men and when they came to the sleeping village he gave an order: "Kill and scalp all Indians, big and little," he shouted, "since nits make lice."

Without warning, every Indian was killed. Afterward scalps were taken and shown to the people in the town.

This story was told many times and everyone feared that the same thing would happen to us. The Long Knives would steal out from their fort and kill us all while we slept. Yet our men did nothing. They sat and shook their heads, but made no plans to defend themselves or their families should the Long Knives come. Even Tall Boy did nothing but talk about the soldiers and how they wanted to see us die.

One day I asked him, "What are you going to do if the Long Knives fall upon us in the night? Will you cover your head and wait to be slain?"

He looked at me and bit his lip. "The gods will tell us what to do," he said. "Now they punish us. When the time comes they will speak and we will hear them."

My father talked this way, too, and many of the other men at Bosque Redondo when summer was ending.

20

Before snow came, when the first north wind blew, my mother and I and my sister started to work, strengthening our hut.

Tall Boy's father knew one of the Long Knives. I think that he gave the soldier a valuable belt of silver and turquoise. Whatever it was, the white man gave him a speckled horse, too old for the soldiers to ride any longer, that they were going to kill. We borrowed this horse and went across the river and cut willow poles, which we used to buttress the thick walls and the sagging roof.

Tall Boy, besides getting the horse for us to use, helped put the poles in place and heap up the earth against them. This pleased my mother. She began to say a word to him now and then and even smiled a little when he was around.

Therefore I was not surprised that Tall Boy's father came over one evening after we finished working on the hut and talked to my father. Then the next day Tall Boy's two uncles came over and talked. The talks went on every day until the new moon and then they made a good marriage bargain, though my mother did not get the old speckled horse, which she wanted.

Relatives came to the wedding. There were so many that all of them could not get inside the hut. Tall Boy went in first, then my father and me. Tall Boy and I sat on a blanket in front of a basket of corn gruel and a jar of water with a ladle. My father crouched nearby. Relatives filed in and sat on both sides of us. Then my father made a cross with white corn pollen over the gruel and a circle around the cross.

First I dipped water with the ladle and poured it over Tall Boy's hands and he did the same to me. Then he dipped a finger into the basket toward the east and ate a pinch of the gruel and I ate a pinch also. We ate pinches from all the different directions. Then the wedding was over and everyone came forward and began to feast.

The elders, as they feasted, gave me advice about being married. One aunt told me not to scold. My unmarried aunt told me to be patient. Two others told me the same thing. My cousin told me to be polite to everyone, even to strangers. There was advice until the relatives left at sundown but I was so excited that I did not hear much of it.

Our hut was too small before Tall Boy moved in with us. Now there was no room, so we made a lean-to of willow poles and earth nearby. It was really more of a cave and in it we stored the things we did not use every day and food if we had more than we needed, which was not often.

Snow came early that year and melted and then a freeze came with a cold wind and the earth was as hard as stone. The white soldiers drove their wagons through the village every week and ladled out flour. But the ladles were smaller than they had been in the summer. Flour always ran low before the wagons came again and people began to go hungry. All but the Apaches, who were fed first.

Once more there was talk that the Long Knives wanted us to die. Before winter was over all the Navahos would starve to death, the old men said.

Snow fell and the wind piled it up around our hut so we had to dig a tunnel to go out. People fell sick and died. Scarcely a day went by that you did not hear a chant for the dead, the wind blowing and the voices singing. Oftentimes it was hard to tell one from the other. It was then, at the time the big snow melted when so many were dying, that I made up my mind.

My husband and I had gone down to the river, using the old speckled horse to gather firewood. After the wood was cut and loaded on the horse, we stood on the bank for a while to get our breath. The gray walls of the fort were the color of the sky and the sky was the color of the land stretching away in the sunless morning. Some soldiers marched up and down, beating on drums and blowing horns.

I said to my husband, "I think of our canyon. I see it before I go to sleep, sometimes in my dreams, and always when I wake up. I see the high stone cliffs and the trees standing against the sky. I see my sheep wandering about with no one to tend them."

"They are not wandering now," he said. "The wolves have killed them and there are none left. You had better think of something else besides sheep."

His words made me angry, though I did not show it. "Some are still alive," I said. "That is why I see them."

He looked at me as if I had turned into a witch. "If some are alive, why is it that I do not see them?" he said. "Do you have a true eye or something that I lack?"

"I suppose I see them because I want to," I said. "And you do not see them because you do not want to."

"I never had any sheep to see," Tall Boy said. "A few goats but no sheep."

"But you can see the canyon if you look," I said. "You were born there and lived there as a boy and grew to be a man. It was your home and it still is."

His long hair was braided into two ropes that lay forward on his chest. He tossed both of them back. "I do not want to think of the canyon," he said.

"My father does not want to think of the canyon either," I said.

"This is not the time to think about the canyon," he said and shouted to the horse.

We climbed the riverbank and set off toward

our hut. The white soldiers were still marching around the fort.

I said nothing more that day about the canyon or the sheep. But I made up my mind as we went back through the village, past the rows of brush huts where people shivered and were dying. Within the rising and waning of five moons my baby would be born.

"It will not be born here, in the shadow of the gray fort," I said to myself, "not here."

21

There was no wool to be found anywhere in the village and when I asked one of the Long Knives if there was wool at the fort he did not answer. I thought that he did not understand Navaho so I made the sign of a blanket and weaving. He sat on a horse, beside the wagon that was bringing us flour. He looked away and said nothing.

Soon afterward I traded my turquoise bracelet for three old blankets of a fine black and white design. By taking one of them apart I was able to save enough thread to repair the other two. The family used them at night, but I took good care of them for they would go with us the day Tall Boy and I left Bosque Redondo.

I was a long time saving food. Every morning when I made the gruel for the family I put two pinches of the flour into a gourd and hid it away in the lean-to. At breakfast I ate two pinches less than the others so things would be even. It took me all the mornings between two moons to fill the gourd, which was enough for a journey of three days.

The next time the wagon came the white soldiers gave us less flour than before and I did not try to save any of it. Still, there was enough for the two of us if we could find some other food along the way. I told Tall Boy about the blankets and the food I had hidden in the lean-to.

"It is a foolish idea that has hold of you," he said. "Before we cross the river they will find our tracks in the snow."

"We can go when the snow melts," I said. "We can go at night in fair weather and leave no tracks for them to find."

He shook his head and looked at me gently, as if he felt pity for me.

"We will talk about it more sometime," he said, turning away.

I knew that he would never think of it again, unless I did. He was like someone who was under a spell. He was like my father, like all the Navaho men, as if he had been forsaken by the gods. But I did not give up my plans for us to flee from Bosque Redondo.

A few days later we borrowed the speckled horse and went down to the river to cut firewood. It was also growing scarce and we had to search to find a tree worth cutting.

We wandered through the river thickets all morning, but had only half a load to show for our work. At noon we went back to where the old horse was tethered. My black dog growled before we got there, and I saw an Apache standing beside the horse.

Tall Boy spoke a greeting. The Indian did not answer. Instead he pointed to the wood on the horse's back.

"Mine," he said. "This wood belong to Apache."

Tall Boy untied the horse, humming a little song to himself, which was a sign that he was angry.

"You get wood on Apache land," said the young Indian. "No good. No like."

He stepped in front of the horse, as if he meant to keep it from moving away. As the horse started to walk around him, he reached out and gave it a blow on the muzzle. The horse had been given many blows in his life from the way he looked and he just stopped and waited. But Tall Boy walked over and took a length of wood down from the horse's back. He gripped it hard in his one good hand.

The Apache had a square chest and spindly legs. He squinted his eyes, which were black as a lizard's, and glanced at the length of wood Tall Boy held in his hand. Then he took a step toward my husband, raising a fist.

Tall Boy struck quickly, as a snake strikes. The blow landed on the Apache's outthrust arm. He dropped the stone he held in his fist. A second blow knocked him off his feet and he fell in the snow and lay there stunned.

We took the horse and went home. I looked back and saw the Apache get to his feet and stagger off. That night while we were eating supper, two soldiers came. They walked into the hut without saying a word and took Tall Boy away. I could not sleep that night thinking about him.

My father went to the fort the next morning and I went with him. There was a big gate in the wall. It was closed and we stood outside in the snow waiting for it to open but no one came all day.

The next morning we went back to the gate. We waited until noon and then it opened and a soldier took us into a courtyard. We waited there until the sun went down. Then a soldier came out and told us to leave but to come back in the morning, which he did.

All morning we walked up and down in the courtyard, trying to keep warm. About noon a Long Knife led us into a room where two men sat. One of them was a soldier and the other a Ute Indian, who told us what the officer said and told him what we answered.

The white officer had blue eyes and a red beard. He wore a hat with a gold cord around it and asked me what my name was.

"Bright Morning," I told him. I did not give him my secret name and he did not ask for it.

"Bright Morning," he said, "tell me what happened when you were gathering wood."

It was bad manners for him to say my name when I was standing there in front of him. But perhaps he did not know this, so I told him everything that happened by the river, as I remembered it.

I said, "Tall Boy is my husband and he is needed at home."

"Mangus the Apache has a home, too, and is needed," the soldier said, "but he has a broken arm and cannot work."

"Neither the riverbank nor the wood that grows there belongs to him," I said. "The arm is his fault."

The officer looked at me sharply with his blue eyes. "Whose fault it is," he said, "is for me to decide, not you."

He began to look at the papers on his desk. The soldier took us to the gate and let us out and we walked home through snow that was beginning to fall.

"What are the Long Knives going to do with him?" I asked my father.

"He has done no wrong," my father answered. "It is not wrong to shield yourself from a man with a stone. They will send him home soon."

22

The snows melted and warm winds blew over Bosque Redondo and green grass began to show along the banks of the river. The big gate at the fort opened every day, the Long Knives marched out, the drums beat, and horns sounded, then the soldiers went back in and the gate closed. I waited every day, but my husband did not come.

With spring settled on the land, the wagons brought more food for us and I was able to save another gourd of flour. We now had enough food to last us on a journey of six days.

Besides the two good blankets, we had a knife, which was like those the soldiers used on the ends of their rifles. I found it on one of the mornings when I went up to the fort. It was wrapped in a cloth and hidden in the grass. I sharpened it on a stone and put it away in the lean-to. The cloth, which was an arm's length of red velvet, would make a girl's small dress or a jacket for a boy.

It was a warm night with many stars and the sound of the river running far away. We had just eaten our supper when Tall Boy came. He walked in so quietly that my black dog did not hear him. He sat down at the fire and ate everything that was left in the pot, hurriedly as if he had never eaten before. He looked gaunt and fearful.

My father said, "Did the Long Knives open the gate for you?"

"They did not open the gate," Tall Boy replied.

"The gate was not open?"

"No."

"But you are here."

"I am here because of a hole in the wall," Tall Boy said, "which I have known about for many weeks."

"Where is this hole you have known about?"

"It is in the place where they cook the food."

"Is it a round hole or one that is square?"

"Neither one nor the other," said Tall Boy. "It is a hole where they shove all the garbage."

"Yes, I have heard of this hole," my father said. "The garbage goes through and falls on the ground outside the wall and the people go there and pick it up."

"That is the hole," Tall Boy said.

"Of a size right for crawling."

"When no one looks. When everyone has left the place where they cook the food."

"And the people have come and carried away all the garbage."

"That is the time," Tall Boy said.

"When will the Long Knives know that you have crawled through the hole?"

"In the morning when they come to cook breakfast."

"Not sooner nor later?"

"Then," my husband said.

He sat staring into the empty pot. I brought him a bowl of corn mush, which he ate in a hurry, and then he fell silent, sitting on his haunches with one arm dangling and the other on his thigh. I thought that he would get up at any moment, that the two of us would flee the camp, but he sat there beside the fire, looking as if he might fall asleep.

"The Long Knives will come in the morning," I said. "You will wake up behind the walls of the fort again."

He glanced at me, blinking his eyes, and I suddenly knew that he had gone as far as he wished to go. He was back with his family. He had eaten our food. He would sleep beside our fire. What happened to him tomorrow did not matter.

He was still blinking at me, halfway between waking and sleeping.

"Are you an old woman?" I asked him.

He stopped blinking.

"An old woman," I went on, my voice rising, "a woman who eats a lot and dozes beside the fire?"

My mother said, "He is worse than an old woman. He is like the old men of the Navahos. All of them."

Tall Boy got to his feet and unhitched his belt, making room for the big supper he had eaten.

My mother looked at him, at his feet. She

would have liked to look him in the face, as she did with me when she was angry. But it was against our tribal law for a mother-in-law to look at her son-in-law this way. She looked at his feet for a long time.

"He will soon have to change his name again," she said. "What do you think it should be? Boy-Who-Sit-at-the-Fire? Boy-Who-Sleeps-Standing-Up? Or something else, like Crawling-Through-a-Hole?"

"I will need time to think hard," I said.

"We shall both think hard," my mother said.

Tall Boy looked at my mother's feet and then at me. He walked slowly around the fire and went outside. I heard him take a deep breath. I stood there and felt like crying. I had not cried since the day we left our home. After a while I sat down beside the fire and cried.

I cried for a long time and nobody tried to stop me. Then Tall Boy came to the doorway and spoke my name and beckoned me to follow him.

When I went outside the first thing I saw was the old speckled horse that belonged to my father-in-law.

"We go now," Tall Boy said.

He made a saddle of the two blankets and tied down the gourds that were filled with flour. The sharp knife he put in his belt.

We did not say good-bye to our family. They knew that we would take their thoughts with us and leave our thoughts for them. Tall Boy got on the horse and we set off through the warm darkness. I had to run to keep pace with him, but when we got to the river he let me climb up behind him.

I untied the two gourds and hung them around my neck to keep them out of the water. My black dog I held in my lap. The river ran swift and cold. As the horse plunged into the water the current swept us out and then back to shore.

On the third try we kept going toward the far shore. We would have drowned except for the old horse. He must have been across the river many times in his life, for he knew how to float with the current and swim if he needed to. There was no moon but all the stars were out, shining on the water.

When we reached the shore, I jumped off the horse and we went along the trail we had used once before. Someday I hoped to have a horse of my own and then I would ride beside my husband. Perhaps he would not own a horse by this time, then it would be he who would have to walk. Across the river the evening fires of Bosque Redondo glowed softly.

We left them far behind, moving along the trail until dawn. Then we made a fire and cooked some mush beside a small lake.

My husband said, "This is the time the Long Knives will find that I have gone. We have the night between us but they will come fast."

"They will not follow us," I said to calm him and

myself. "There are thousands of Indians at Bosque Redondo. Will the Long Knives bother to look for one? And if they do, which way will they go? If they do anything, it will be to search the village. Our friends will tell them nothing."

We slept until the sun was high and awakened to the barking of my black dog. There were soldiers on the trail. By putting our ears to the earth we could hear the steps of their horses. But they came from the west. From our hiding place we watched them pass, driving a small band of Navahos toward Bosque Redondo.

Tall Boy pulled the knife from his belt and I think that he would have rushed out and attacked the soldiers alone if I had not pleaded with him. As it was, we made so much noise that one of the Long Knives stopped his horse and looked in our direction before he rode on.

We left the small lake and rode to the northwest, but we had not gone far when my husband said, "There are places closer than Canyon de Chelly where we can hide. These places are safer also. The Long Knives do not watch them like they watch the canyon."

"But the canyon is our home," I said. "We have lived there. We know where wood is and water and food. The sheep. What of the sheep?"

I was walking beside him and he glanced down at me in scorn. "Sheep? They are eaten by the wolves, as I have told you," he said. "If not, if there are some left, what do we do with them?

Where can we graze them that they will not be seen by the Long Knives?"

"We will be careful where we graze them," I said. "There are hidden places that I know."

He shrugged his shoulders, which he did when he did not want to talk about something, and fell silent.

We went on for six suns, ate the last of our flour and then snared rabbits and squirrels. I was certain that my husband had decided to go to Canyon de Chelly, after all.

But on the seventh day Tall Boy left the trail and we went northward over a ridge into wooded, rolling country. He had hunted there once and called it Elk-Running Valley.

A stream ran down from the high mountains and wandered through a meadow until it came to a dam beavers had made from brush and trees. There the stream backed up and formed a small pond with grassy banks. We built a hut beside the pond and lived in it through the summer. It was here that my son was born.

After that, Tall Boy brought down poles from the high country, dragging them behind the speckled horse. He made the hut larger and strengthened the roof for winter snow. He fashioned a throwing stick and killed two young deer. He was busy all the time hunting or making something. He still could not use his injured arm, but he had become quick and skillful with the other one. He no longer seemed to think about his injury.

I was busy, too. I worked the deer hides with a

bone scraper and softened them in my mouth and made a pair of leggings for my son. I also made him a jacket out of the velvet I had saved and a heavy coat from a beaver pelt. Yet not a day went by that summer or when the snows came that I did not think of my sheep.

23

One morning early in the spring, while we were eating breakfast, soldiers appeared on the ridge. Our lean-to was hidden among the pine trees and could not be seen from where they stood. Nor could they see the speckled horse, which was tethered beyond the lean-to. We felt uneasy, nonetheless.

The Long Knives came down from the ridge, riding fast. We were ready to flee but they turned away from us and headed into the south.

"The Long Knives will travel for one day, no longer," Tall Boy said. "I have been in the canyon where they are going and they cannot get through. They will have to turn back. We can look for them tomorrow."

We finished eating our breakfast. The spring sun was warm. Beaver were working on their dam, cutting brush on the banks and swimming across the pond with it. Tall Boy sat with his son in his lap and watched them for a long time going back and forth.

Then we loaded the old horse with our clothes and some dried deer meat and left Elk-Running

Valley before the sun was high. We kept off the trail the soldiers had used.

At the top of the ridge we went north and west. It was in the direction of our canyon, but I was afraid to ask my husband whether we were going there or not. If we were, then it would be better not to ask him. Sometimes, if he was asked too many questions, he would change his mind and do something else.

I was not certain that we were going home until on the evening of the fifth day I saw the high ramparts against the northern sky. They were crimson in the setting sun, even the tall trees along their edges were crimson. I felt like shouting and dancing, like running around in circles, as I always did when I was very happy. But I walked quietly through the spring grass as if I saw nothing there in the sky.

Tall Boy was riding in front of me. He spoke and pointed into the north.

"Yes," I said calmly.

"We go because I am tired of hearing about sheep," he said. "And for no other reason. It is a dangerous place to go. There are no sheep left, but still I go. If there is one left it will be shaggy like a buffalo and so wild you will have to catch it in a trap. But I go because I am tired of the sheep talk. Oh, Coyote Brothers in the far and near hills, I am tired of sheep."

He nudged the speckled horse and rode on, out of sight.

My son was strapped to a carrying board slung

over my back. I stopped and took him out of the harness and held him in my arms. The crimson ramparts had changed to gold and a gold mist drifted over the sky. I turned his head so that he faced the stone cliffs as they changed to purple and the first star came out.

The next morning Tall Boy left to go into the canyon. He wanted to find out if any of the Long Knives were camped there or if other tribes, the Apaches or the Utes, had come while we were gone. The old horse had grown slow and lame, so he left it behind and went on foot. In two days he returned, carrying a braided rope, which he had picked up somewhere, and two horseshoes.

"I saw no Indians," he said, while we were breaking camp. "No signs of the Long Knives. Nothing has changed.

After a time, not right away, I asked, "Did you see any of my sheep?"

"One," he said, "on the trail to the mesa. It had more hair than a buffalo. At first I thought it was a buffalo."

"It has not been shorn for a long time," I said.

"Nor will it be shorn soon," my husband answered. "It is wilder than a mountain sheep. You will have to catch it in a trap. But after you catch it, how you will shear it I do not know."

"I have shears," I said. "I hid them in the cave when we left."

"You hid many things," Tall Boy said.

"We will need many things," I answered.

The river ran full. Blue snow water brimmed

over the banks and flowed into the meadow. The cornfield was the same field the Long Knives had left. The peach trees, which they had stripped of bark, stood in black rows. Our hogan was still a ring of gray ashes and tumbled weeds. We stopped there and talked, deciding where we would go.

"The high mesa is safe," my husband said. "But if the Long Knives come we will be cut off from water, like we were before."

"From water and from the sheep," I said.

"What sheep?" Tall Boy asked. "The one that looks like a buffalo?"

"There is a small canyon where the river forks," I said. "I have been there with my sheep. It has grass and a spring comes out of a rock. It is hidden from the big canyon so that you can pass by and not know it is there."

"Let us go then to this place," Tall Boy said.

I started off, leading the way along the river, to the big rocks that stood at the entrance to the hidden canyon. The rocks and the gnarled sycamores that grew among them formed a low, winding corridor and Tall Boy had to climb down from the horse to get through.

Hidden Canyon was just as I remembered it. The yellow cliffs rose on all sides. The spring flowed from the rock and made a waterfall that the wind caught and spun out over the meadow. On the far side of the meadow was the grove of wild plums, where I had picked many handfuls of fruit. The trees now were covered with white and pink blossoms.

But I had forgotten the cave. Tall Boy saw it at once.

"A good place," he said and went off to explore it.

The cave was on the face of the western cliff, where the morning sun shone first. It was about thirty feet from the ground and twice that many feet in width. To reach it there were handholds cut into the soft, yellow stone, but some were worn away and I had never tried to use them. Indians had lived there a long time ago and left, no one knew why.

Tall Boy started to chip away at the handholds, using the knife I had found at Bosque Redondo. He dug out four of the holds and tried them. I held my breath, I feared that he would never be able to make his way up the face of the cliff. Even with two good hands it was not easy. But he went up and came down without trouble.

"See," he said to his son, "it is easy. Before long you will be able to climb. For your mother, we will stretch a rope which she can hold on to."

Clouds were gathering and he started working on the handholds again. While I watched him my black dog pointed his ears and I heard a small noise. It came from the far side of the meadow, near the wild plum trees, and I walked in that direction.

I had not gone far when out of the tall grass I saw a ewe looking at me. She turned away as I reached her, but did not flee. Her coat was thick and full of burrs. Beside her was a lamb, not more than a few days old.

I took my son from his carrying board and held him up so that he could see the lamb. He wanted to touch it, but with both hands he was grasping a toy which his father had given him, a willow spear tipped with stone. Tall Boy had made up a song about the Long Knives and how the spear would kill many of them. Every night he sang this song to his son.

I took the spear and dropped it in the grass and stepped upon it, hearing it snap beneath my foot.

My son touched the lamb once before the two moved away from us. He looked up at me and laughed and I laughed with him.

Rain had begun to fall. It made a hissing sound in the tall grass as we started toward the cave high up in the western cliff. Tall Boy had finished the steps and handholds and now stood under the cave's stone lip, waving at us.

I waved back at him and hurried across the meadow. I raised my face to the falling rain. It was Navaho rain.

Postscript

Sing Down the Moon is based upon two years, 1863 to 1865, in the history of the Navaho Indians. Before this time many treaties were made between the Navahos and the United States. Most of them were broken, some by the whites, some by the Indians.

In June 1863 the United States sent Colonel Kit Carson through the Navaho country, centered in what is now northeastern Arizona, with instructions to destroy all crops and livestock. At the head of 400 soldiers, Carson pillaged the land, pursued fleeing bands of Navahos, and killed those who fought back. He asked help from the Utes, traditional enemies of the Navahos, promising them the livestock, the women, and the children they captured.

Word was sent out that all Navahos were to give themselves up, and early in 1864 they began to surrender. By March they had started on their long journey to Fort Sumner, 180 miles southeast of Santa Fe, New Mexico. A total of 8491 reached the fort. A few small groups hid like beasts in the depths of the Grand Canyon, on the heights of the Black Mesa, and other inaccessible places.

This 300-mile journey of the Navahos is known as The Long Walk. To this day, Navaho men and women speak of it with bitterness. And if you talk to a Navaho child for more than a few minutes he will tell you the story. He has heard it in the cradle and learned it at his mother's knee.

The Navahos were held prisoners at Fort Sumner until 1868. Late in that year they were set free, each with a gift of a sheep and a goat. Poorly clothed to meet the coming winter, without horses or wagons, they left on foot. Their new home was a wilderness located in the Four Corners country, a sandy, wind-swept desert of little rain. It was near the Canyon de Chelly (pronounced "shay"), where the states of Utah, Arizona, Colorado, and New Mexico touch.

The massacre that Bright Morning speaks about was led by a preacher named J. M. Chivington. With a company of volunteers he rode out from Denver in 1864 and set upon a sleeping village of Arapahos and Cheyennes, killing everyone—75 men, 225 old people, women, and children.

Some 1500 Navahos died at Fort Sumner from smallpox and other diseases. But the group who survived has grown to more than 100,000. The Navahos wanted to live. Like Bright Morning, they thirsted for life. They still do. You will see girls who look much like her, tending their sheep now in Canyon de Chelly. They are dressed in velveteen blouses, a half-dozen ruffled and flounced petticoats, their hair tied in chignons—a style copied from the officers' wives at Fort Sumner long ago.